Praise for *The Circumferen*

"Brilliant and bizarre, Lavie Tidhar's *World* is many things—but fundamentally it is a love letter to the Golden Age of science fiction, whether or not it deserves it (it does), as well as a love letter to its writers, whether or not they deserve it."
—Molly Tanzer, author of *Vermilion* and *Creatures of Will and Temper*

"Ingeniously constructed and stylistically protean, this seven-course banquet of a novel glistens with the Golden Age of science fiction, even as it nourishes our neurons with a marvelous thought experiment: What if an amalgam of Philip K. Dick and L. Ron Hubbard had founded a religion that, against all odds, provided a gateway into ultimate reality?"
—James Morrow, award-winning author of *Shambling Towards Hiroshima*

"Tidhar wins it all with this magnificently original mind-bender of a novel about a missing husband and a mysterious book that disappears as soon as you read it. *The Circumference of the World* is two parts Philip K. Dick, two parts Brothers Strugatsky, and six parts blow your f**king mind."
—Junot Díaz, author of *The Brief Wondrous Life of Oscar Wao*

"I always have been partial to dangerous books, and to fictions about dangerous books, and the one at the swirling center of this exhilarating tour de force is a doozy—just like every book by Lavie Tidhar."
—Andy Duncan, three-time World Fantasy Award winner

"Reading a new Lavie Tidhar novel is always a treat. You can count on engaging prose paired with an inventive story, and *The Circumference of the World* certainly fits that bill."
—*The Speculative Shelf*

Praise for Lavie Tidhar

On *Neom*

"A stunning return to his world of *Central Station*, twinning the fates of humans and robots alike at a futuristic city on the edge of the Red Sea."
—*Green Man Review*

"This is Tidhar at his best: the crazily proliferating imagination, the textures, the ideas, the dazzling storytelling. A brilliant portrait of community and its possibilities."
—Adam Roberts, author of *Purgatory Mount*

"This was superb, and I'm in awe of Tidhar's vision. He's conjured up a futuristic city that feels simultaneously ultramodern and also run-down."
—*The Speculative Shelf*

"Yet again, Lavie Tidhar's future world of *Neom* is exciting and distinctive, his characters complex and fascinating, and his themes powerful and thought-provoking."
—Kij Johnson, author of *The River Bank*

"Vivid and techno-mythological, *Neom* infects you with something special that transcends all the incidents and terrors—a shimmering current of guarded optimism."
—David Brin, author of *Existence*, *Earth*, and *The Postman*

"Always expect the unexpected with Lavie Tidhar, and this welcome return to the sprawling space-operatic world of *Central Station* delivers oodles of poetry, action, memorable characters, wonderfully bizarre landscapes and wild imagination."
—Maxim Jakubowski, author of *The Piper's Dance*

On *Central Station*

"Beautiful, original, a shimmering tapestry of connections and images."
—Alastair Reynolds, author of the *Revelation Space* series

"A dazzling tale of complicated politics and even more complicated souls. Beautiful."
—Ken Liu, author of *The Paper Menagerie* and *The Grace of Kings*

[STARRED] "Readers of all persuasions will be entranced."
—*Publishers Weekly*

[STARRED] "A fascinating future glimpsed through the lens of a tight-knit community."
—*Library Journal*

Selected Titles by Lavie Tidhar

The Bookman (2010)
Osama (2011)
The Violent Century (2013)
A Man Lies Dreaming (2014)
Central Station (2016)
Candy (2018)
Unholy Land (2018)
Adler (2020, graphic novel series with Paul McCaffery)
By Force Alone (2020)
The Escapement (2021)
The Hood (2021)
Maror (2022)
Neom (2022)

Lavie Tidhar
The Circumference of the World

The Circumference of the World
Copyright © 2023 by Lavie Tidhar

Interior and cover design by Elizabeth Story

Tachyon Publications LLC
1459 18th Street #139
San Francisco, CA 94107
415.285.5615
www.tachyonpublications.com
tachyon@tachyonpublications.com

Series editor: Jacob Weisman
Project editors: Jill Roberts and Jaymee Goh

Print ISBN: 978-1-61696-362-0
Digital ISBN: 978-1-61696-363-7

Printed in the United States by Versa Press, Inc.

First Edition: 2023
9 8 7 6 5 4 3 2 1

LAVIE TIDHAR

THE CIRCUMFERENCE
OF THE WORLD

TACHYON
SAN FRANCISCO

WE CAN START THIS ANYWHERE. With Oskar Lens, with Daniel, even with Delia Welegtabit, who is Occluded from us yet tantalizingly close, her scent, her taste on our tongues, her shadow at the edge of our vision.

We pick a moment, almost at random. A moment like a spider bite, twisting jagged lines run from it, under the skin, the blind grubs hatching and making their way into a world they've yet to learn. The lines extrude from that single point of origin, making us think of a child's drawing of a star.

Time for us is omnidirectional. And so we follow one strand, back along the axis from present to past.

Just remember: none of this is real.

PART ONE

STORIAN SMOL BLONG DELIA WELEGTABIT

1.

In the wet season the rain falls in drops as fat as butterflies and the islands singaot to each other across the water in the language of the bubu and tamat, ol olfala blong yumi.

It was on the island of Vanua Lava that Delia Welegtabit was born. It happened at the time that the French man came to Sola with his pet crocodiles.

The French man was a friend of the master. He came by ship and he brought with him two pet crocodiles of the kind common in the Solomon Islands that lie to the northwest. The crocodiles were very small and the men could play with them. When they tired of playing, the men put the crocodiles into a large drum filled with water. In the night the rain fell and the tank overflowed and in the morning the crocodiles were gone.

It was at the precise moment that the tank overflowed and the crocodiles escaped to their freedom that Delia's mother, Serendipity, gave a cry of pain. The light from the hurricane lamp scattered shadows on her face. She was on her knees on the mattress by the fire. Dry wood was stacked three feet high and two feet deep along the wall. Embers glowed in the hol blong faea dug into the earth in place of a hearth. The puskat was gnawing on the last of the fish bones in one corner of the hut. The only real illumination came from the hurricane lamp.

Serendipity's husband, Roger, squatted beside her, his face matted with sweat.

"Push," he said softly. "Push."

Waves of pain washed over Serendipity, corresponding, or perhaps responding, to the waves of the Pacific Ocean as they broke against the nearby shore. The tide was coming in. The rain beat against the ocean like a drum.

Serendipity stared into the formless dark as though she could discern shapes moving on the water. A full moon was hidden behind the clouds and in its ghostly light the volcano was seen in mere outline, a suggestion of a force both patient and awake. Its spumes of steam joined the everclouds, obscuring the hill of the dead beyond.

Let this one be healthy, she thought. Against the sky a storm petrel flew high, riding the wind.

"Push."

In Bislama, a melange of English, some French, and the untold word-shoals of Melanesian tongues, the word is "pusum," as in "pusum kenu"—to row a canoe across the water. Years later, Delia would search in vain for the music of Bislama in the accented Englishes of a dozen worlds each day in her passage through London, searching for the cadences and rhythm of a language few even knew existed, and she never found it. Its absence would eat at her heart without reason, she would be startled while shopping on the Whitechapel Road by the call of a vendor hawking breadfruit, which must have travelled a vast distance, like her, to end up ignobly in this shabby market with the smell of car exhausts and the tinny beat of Hindi music, but whenever she asked, more in rote than in faith, no one had ever heard of her home, and no one knew of a place called Vanuatu.

The pain rang through Serendipity like the thrum of a great bell being struck. The pressure built inside her, like a desperate need to go to the smolhaos, a need to defecate. The baby pressed against her bowels. Behind her the midwife, Mrs. Atkin, grunted wordlessly and her fingers went within.

"I gud, i gud," she said. "Bebe i stap kam—" The baby is coming.

Blood pooled on the dry earth between Serendipity's legs. She moaned in a low unearthly voice. She felt something give. Mrs. Atkin patted her on the small of the back, distractedly.

"Gud, gud," she said.

She watched the head emerge. She had seen so many babies born over the decades, in huts like these, in rain like this, so many tiny upside-down human beings emerging into tenuous life, but it never failed to move an anxious spot within her, like an old injury that niggled still.

Why did they do it? she wondered. It was an awful, blind determination of those newborn passengers to depart the hull of their ship for an unknown, unknowable world to explore. The missionaries said Jesus, and Jesus was great indeed, but he was a man whatever else he was, and not a woman, and therefore never carried in his hold, like a ship across the sea, a hatching life. She herself had now traversed the great arc of a life, from wriggling newborn to old age—she was too old, really, to be kneeling here, on the hard ground, at this hour of the night, but how could she refuse this front seat at the act of creation?—and soon she would descend the arc to its final termination point. And what then?

But right then the little head slid out farther and Roger cried out and Serendipity pushed herself against the earth until she lay almost flattened and with her behind raised in the air and Mrs. Atkin took hold of the baby, gently, firmly, anchoring it into reality, and it came out in one single rush and she said, "It's a girl."

The little thing still trailed its lifeline back into its mother. Mrs. Atkin looked at Roger and then shook her head and cut the cord herself. The girl opened her mouth and took in air for the first time into her lungs.

She screamed.

Serendipity rolled over, exhausted. She lay on the mattress and Mrs. Atkin placed Delia on her chest. Serendipity looked at the baby and held her. She'd had seven children and four had lived.

"She's alive," she said.

Mrs. Atkin watched mother and child. The baby was white against her mother's black skin. She was a waetwoman blong Bankis, that is to say, an albino, like her brother Denden or like Mrs. Atkin herself, for albinos were common in the Banks Islands of the New Hebrides. And though some, like that uneducated Mrs. Moses from the store, said that they smelled different when it rained, it was nonsense—though their skin burned easily, and they often suffered problems with their eyes.

This was how Delia Welegtabit came into the world, though we do not know how she departed it. It is said that some one hundred billion human souls had been born on the planet Earth before Delia came to be. A hundred billion naked blind explorers emerging into moonlight and rain, icefall and sun, a hundred billion little hearts beating across time. She was the evolutionary product of a race that had survived an ice age and the decline of all its rival human species; that had invented farming, tools, architecture, war, and history itself, which is the art of writing down things that happened.

The missing crocodiles, having slithered across the grass and into the trees, made their way through huts and stores and found at last, on the other end of Sola, a quiet river. It smelled of sulphur and its water was warm, but fish swam between the rocks and fat naura scuttled in the shallows. The crocodiles could smell others of their kind, but the smell was distant. They slid into the water and disappeared into the river's breadth.

Serendipity held her daughter and cried.

Time occupied Delia's thoughts, its mystery, its very essence. "I was born in the time the French man's crocodiles escaped," she would say, "I was born when the moon is fulap." The thought of her birth fascinated her. She *was*, she knew that, she thought herself alive. And yet, before, she was not, a scant five years earlier there had been no Delia, not even the thought of Delia, and yet the world existed, time passed, the moon continued to rise and fall, indifferent.

At five years old she was a curious if quiet child. Her schooling was conducted in French, but she had shown an aptitude mostly for numbers, which require no language but themselves. She could climb, frog-like, the tall, slender coconut trees; knew how to use a bush knife to hack branches and split open the outer layering of the nut to reveal the green hidden centre; knew its face, which was a snake's face, three soft, tri-angulated spots which could be cored for the water inside to be drunk; she knew how to catch the solwota crabs in the shallows, how to gut a fish, how to push a canoe and how to solve a simultaneous equation.

At home they spoke Bislama, since her father was from Ambai and her mother from Motlap and neither spoke the other's tongue. Delia's white skin blistered easily, and black freckles crept up on her nose and cheeks. Five years can pass quickly, though each day is self-contained and whole and seems to last forever. Even for us time is a mystery, though we live in the well where time trickles to a crawl and, at the bottom, at last fractures.

In Vanuatu, as elsewhere on Earth, time can be mea-sured by the fattening of the moon, its rise and its absence, as much as it can be measured by clocks. It was that moon's face that Delia missed, sometimes terribly, when living in London. On the islands the moon was a constant, and at five years of age Delia would spend hours on the grassy field by the copra storage sheds, where the boys would play fut-bol on a Sunday after church, and gaze up at the night sky. For the view from the islands is not the view from the city, marred by artificial light and obscured by pollution. Lying on her back in that field in Sola, in the moonless dark, she could look up to see the entire Milky Way galaxy spread out from horizon to horizon, a fog of dense stars, as deceptive as spider silk. Somewhere there is our home, too, though you wouldn't see it.

And on those nights when the moon came out and the galaxy diminished in its reflective light, Delia studied it intently. She studied it like a face in the mirror, for the face of the moon to her was that of an albino child, a white glow upon which the ravages of time and meteors are described in black freckles, and she saw, at least, something of herself in it. She wanted to visit it; to step upon its dusty soil; to examine its rocks and walk in the folds of its canyons and craters, and gaze upwards into the black sky and see the earth rise, a blue-white planet on which the island of Vanua Lava was no more than a volcanic speck of rock in the midst of a vast and featureless ocean.

In London she missed the moon; its glow; the way it marked time; its great invisible gravitational influence on the ocean, which pushed and pulled the sea with its tides; its face, which in her child's imagination took on the face of God, immense and unknowable, yet always there, and always looking down, without judgement or compassion. In London it was always hidden behind something, one could go years and not know Earth had a lunar companion at all.

At five her best friend was Denden, who at six was closest to her age. Together they ran like white ghosts through thick forest, dove for lobsters in the deeps of Sanara, wove traps for birds. Together they explored the small island, Lenoh, which jutted just off the coast of Mosina. Hushed, they walked through this microscopic universe where the trees grew wild. It was uninhabited by humans, colonised by ants, who in silence swarmed over the mulch and among the roots on their inexplicable errands. The canopy of the trees grew thick and a cool gloom pervaded the island's interior. Beyond it lay the black rocks called Qat's Canoe, and if one followed the coastline one would eventually reach Sanara and the point, after which the Bay of Sola began.

Delia went out on the rocks and watched the ocean spray as the water beat against the rocks. Exposed in the sun, coconuts lay drying and she darted out from the cover of the trees and picked one, two, three, examining them minutely, like a connoisseur.

Satisfied, she darted back and went to Denden. He sat cross legged and still and the ants amended their course to take him into account, and formed a small dark moving half-circle that skirted the whiteness of his feet.

They broke open the coconuts. Navara was their favourite delicacy, and they tore it out in chunks and chewed happily, for it was very sweet. And when they were done, Delia told him the story of Qasavara, the Man Eater, and of Qat, the trickster who bested him.

Then, as night fell, they crossed the deepening gulf of water that in high tide separated the small island of Lenoh from the beach at Mosina. And they began to wander down the long shoreline, stepping nimbly over the wet hard sand, following a trail through the scattered village.

For Mosina was once a village whose houses lay close together, but an earthquake had rent the island asunder some decades back, in that long and impossible time that existed before Delia was born; it had stolen in the night and torn open the ground, and the people of Mosina fled, and some were swallowed by the earth and others watched them and were helpless, and after that the village was rebuilt along the shore and the houses were set far apart from each other.

"It tore the ground open like an envelope," Delia heard her father say once, though she could not remember when or where. But the words, his intonation, remained within her, stored in her memory even as her cells replaced themselves, as she became another and another, a succession of Delias throughout the years: the memory, the words, his voice, were encoded as a series of flashing neurons that themselves were replaced again and again. The data survived while the storage medium changed.

But why? Why this sentence? It came to her unbidden, at inappropriate times. Queuing up for a coffee at a stall in Borough Market under the arches of London Bridge, in the early morning, with frost covering the brick stones and her breath rising ghostly and white in the air, the loose change cold in her palm, she thought of it. He meant that a force tore it with great ease. A quake, an explosion of energy for which the island was incidental, a detail in its path. It tore up the ground without discrimination, trees and huts. It came from the ocean and the ocean flooded into the rent in the land.

She thought of it sometimes in the small apartment that she shared with Levi, when the postman had come and gone, his feet echoing on the carpetless corridor outside, and the mail dropped through the letterbox with a noise greater than it should have been, as if to signify how far it'd come, how important it was. And she'd hold an envelope, it could have been a catalogue, a letter from the university, a phone bill, and as she tore it open she would think of her father and his voice would come back to her or, rather, an echo of his voice, a simulacrum existed now only in her mind, a vui haunting, formed of flashing neurons.

But she seldom thought of that day on the small island. And of how, as they walked past, she came to a hut and heard a low and painful moan from inside it, and saw her father, Roger, milling outside with some others. And so she went and hugged him and he lifted Delia up and held her in his arms, and the low moaning sound continued.

"It's Mrs. Atkin," Roger said. "Do you remember her, Delia? She was there when you were born. She helped you come out."

"Is she ill?" Delia said, secretly resenting the suggestion she needed help doing anything, and her father said, "Mrs. Atkin is old, and she is dying. Do you want to see her?"

Delia was not at all sure she did, but Roger took her with him anyway. Men outside were preparing kava, peeling the grey straggly roots and chopping the bitter flesh with their knives, and women stood and chatted, with their children pressed against their long island dresses. In the distance Delia could see the blue-green outline of the great island to the west, which was Espiritu Santo.

Then they all disappeared as Roger ducked under the low awning and they entered Mrs. Atkin's hut.

It was a hut with woven bamboo walls and a thatched natangura roof, though the base had been made with cement, making it what they called a semi-permanent structure. It was lit by a candle burning on a low table and the flame flickered with the air coming in through the open door and cast shadows that moved on the walls like the black-and-white water snakes sacred to the islands. Mrs. Atkin lay on the floor on a woven mat, her chest rising and falling painfully and unevenly, and it put young Delia in mind of the earthquake again, and of the land rising and falling as though it were in pain; sometimes in London she would awaken from a sleep, disoriented, the fog of a woman-earthquake monstrosity dissipating in her mind, and she would listen to the traffic and the footsteps and drunken song of passersby and take comfort in the yellow light off the street that invaded her and Levi's bedroom from the outside. It is early in life that nightmares are made, though Delia was not scared, not then: all that she saw was an old woman dying.

A curious half-moan, half-whistle rose from Mrs. Atkin's throat and passed her lips and escaped, each painful, valued breath expelled and another taken in with a gasping, shuddering breath, and it was that sound, mechanical and faulty, that shaped itself eventually into the monster of Delia's dream: for her monsters were partially influenced by the Japanese movies she had discovered, much later, during her studies in Suva, in Fiji, and Mrs. Atkin's ghost marched across Vanua Lava as a giant robot would, its thudding steps crushing sacred rocks and nakamals and huts, tearing trees and altering the course of rivers, and making the earth shake and tremble uncontrollably.

"Mrs. Atkin," Roger said, gently. "It's me, Roger. I brought Delia with me. You remember Delia, don't you, Mrs. Atkin? You delivered her, five years ago?"

Mrs. Atkin never spoke, all the time they were inside. Delia wasn't sure she was conscious of their being there. She seemed far away, yet not in peace. She struggled against something unseen. Each breath was a battle, won at a cost, but won fairly, and treasured.

"Daddy, can she hear us?" Delia said.

"I don't know," Roger said. Mrs. Atkin hissed, a life escaping like gas. Delia snuggled into her father's arms. He held her with ease, she was lighter than a bag of copra. Outside, night had descended, and with it a kind of hush, and

15

she could smell the fires burning and hear the men hawking phlegm as they drank the kava and it began to take effect.

"We had better go," Roger said. "Goodbye, Mrs. Atkin."

"Goodbye, Mrs. Atkin . . . lukim yu bakegen," Delia murmured.

"I hope so," Roger said, softly. "But perhaps not on this side of Surevuvu."

And he carried Delia outside.

Light suffused Delia's days. It was new-born light travelling from the sun, bouncing off the moon, transmuting through the atmosphere, bouncing off trees, flowers, people, ocean, canoes, cargo boats, desks, books, soap, mats, and shells. Her eyes were sensitive to the light, she wore dark shades her father bought for her on a rare visit to Port Vila, which lay many miles and islands away. It slowed down the light's passage and filtered it. At night she took off the shades and watched old, ancient light, which had formed in distant alien stars hundreds and thousands and millions of years away, long taem bifo, bifo, had travelled through vacuum and interstellar dust and finally touched, gently, the lens of her eyes and was converted to a signal that travelled into her brain and became, at last, vision.

At thirteen light fell on the books in the school library. They were books more mouldy than dusty, for the air of Vanua Lava was humid and the books old, and had come a long way. They were donations from Ostrelia, mostly, the unwanted discards of well-meaning folk who lived in houses as strange and alien as starships.

The coconut plantation of Sola was no more. In 1980 the New Hebrides declared independence from their joint colonial masters of France and England, and became Vanuatu. The master left; the copra rotted on the wharf uncollected. Roger lost his job when the plantation shut down, but Sola was now designated capital of the newly-minted province of the Banks and Torres islands, Torba, and he became accountant for the province. Delia's oldest brother, Jonah, just returned from three-year service as a policeman on Tanna, became the chief constable for the province, and preened constantly at his newfound importance and elevated station. The administration was now based in the complex of offices and abandoned storage units that had formed the plantation's heart, and in many ways things continued as before.

But of the books, one in particular left a special impression on Delia and would, much later, be the cause of Levi's disappearance and, *much* later, give us some cause for bemusement of our own.

This book did not come from the school's library of donated books, but rather had been in the possession of the Welegtabit family, though it had not come from Roger's line but from Serendipity's; her father, so family lore went, had been an American soldier. We are bemused because the book should not have existed, and but for the memories here archived (though this word not quite mean the same to you as it does to us), there is no real proof that it ever has. For human memory is imperfect at best, and our reconstruction of it liable to error.

The cover of the book depicted a swirling cloud of stars, sucked inexorably in nebula whorls, towards a malevolent black eye that dominated the centre of the page.

The title, *Lode Stars*, was etched above it.

The book was published in America, in 1962. Its heroine was herself called Delia.

The name of the author was Eugene Charles Hartley.

2.

"But I don't understand," Levi said. They sat in a coffee shop in the maze of streets by Spitalfields. His long, thin fingers moved constantly, nervously; he often bit his nails; Delia sometimes wished he'd smoke, just so he'd have something to occupy his hands. Instead he held a pen, when he remembered to carry one, scribbling equations on napkins, receipts, other people's business cards: whatever paper he could lay his hands on. "I don't understand, she just lay there?"

"She was dying, Levi."

"But you'd seen dead people before, you told me so, Delia. People die all the time."

"But I never saw anyone *dying*," Delia said. She stared into her hot chocolate. "Death is nothing, it's an absence, a collection of decaying cells. Dying is different, it's an act, a process."

"Decay is a process."

"You're being obtuse."

"And you're being morbid." He lifted his espresso to his lips. She used to love his lips. The first time they kissed was under the lions in Trafalgar Square, their second date. It rained. His lips were warm and full. His fingers traced formulas onto her back.

"I shouldn't have said anything."

"I think I'm close," Levi said. Changing the subject to himself was his favourite conversational gambit. "I've almost got it, Delia. The equations."

She drank but the chocolate was warm and cloying. "You're almost thirty," she said, cruelly. It was taboo for her to say it. Funny, how the word came from the languages of the islands. Her life had been bound by taboo, tambou. But his face closed to her. His eyes no longer saw her. As she knew he would react; she had said it with purpose.

"Levi, I'm sorry—"

"But you're not."

"Levi, you can't explain everything, you can't—"

"You call yourself a mathematician?" he said. Sneered.

"I am not as good as you—"

"No," he said. "You're not."

The silence pooled between them. Outside it rained but it was London rain, cold and drizzly, nothing like the warm downpours of her home. She thought of volcanic islands rising out of the sea. Outside, office men hurried with dark umbrellas.

"She died three days later and her spirit went to Surevuvu," Delia said.

"Your midwife?"

"Yes, my midwife."

"What's Surevuvu?"

"It's the hill of the dead, behind the volcano. It's where the dead go."

"Obviously."

"But isn't this what your equations are all about, Levi?

Ghosts and where they go?"

"Information, Delia. We're all just complexes of information, of data. It's all in the book—"

"Your stupid book!"

"You're just spoiling for a fight today. Anyway you told me you knew it. You saw it, with your own eyes. You saw *Lode Stars*."

"It was just a paperback novel, Levi. It was just a silly sci-fi book."

"To think you had it in your hands."

"I read, Levi. I read books and I studied numbers and I preferred numbers. Fiction is silly. And anyway you are talking about physics, not mathematics."

"Enough!" He was angry. She didn't know why she was trying to rile him. He'd been distant all summer, absorbed in his research—she tried to follow his math but she couldn't. Either she wasn't smart enough—or the equations were all wrong. He was almost thirty and thirty was a fatal number for mathematicians.

Ramanujan, dead at twenty; Einstein publishing his *Theory of Relativity* aged twenty-six; Gauss writing his epic *Disquisitiones Arithmeticae* by the age of twenty-one. Levi, by contrast, taught mathematics to undergraduates at a private university catering to American study-abroads; was almost thirty; and his social life revolved around fortnightly meetings with a group of kindred sci-fi fans in a pub in Holborn.

She knew with quiet despair that he wasn't going to make it. And she knew with quiet despair that he knew it too.

————

They had books in common, to begin with.

They'd met five years back, at a university social. She was older than him but she didn't mind and neither did he. He was tall, gawky, never still, with a confidence back then that was almost arrogance. He had smiled more easily. He drank very occasionally but he had been tipsy that night.

"What's your favourite number?" was the first thing he'd said to her.

Delia laughed, taken aback.

"Don't think," he said, "just say the first thing that comes into your head."

"Six."

"Carbon," he said, immediately.

"Yes."

"The basis of all life on Earth."

"Yes."

"But that's physics, not mathematics," he said, and she said, "Yes."

"I like you," he said, suddenly and inexplicably, and again she laughed.

"Because I said six?"

"No," he said, and smiled, a little goofily. He offered her his hand and she shook it solemnly. "Levi Armstrong," he said. "Lecturer in undergraduate mathematics." He made a face.

"Delia Welegtabit," she said, and, "I know."

"Oh," he said. He sounded pleased. So Delia explained how she'd recently joined the faculty as an assistant, and how she'd seen him around, and that she was from Vanuatu originally ("Where?" he'd said, and she'd said, "It's an archipelago of islands in the South Pacific, near the Solomon Islands," and Levi nodded and said, "Ah, yes, of course, the *Solomon* Islands, the Solomon *Islands*," with a serious expression and made her laugh) and they got to talking and she said, "But you didn't say what *your* favourite number is—" though she didn't care, really, it wasn't something she thought of.

"C," Levi said, promptly.

"The speed of light in vacuum?"

"Aha."

She was feeling tipsy herself. The social was coming to a close, professors and colleagues departing with unsteady steps. "Coming to the pub?" she said.

"Well, I don't usually—" then he seemed to catch himself, ran his fingers through his thick hair, smiled self-consciously. "Sure."

They joined the others, put on their coats, trudged through air as cold and wet as a January birthday to the pub across the road. Delia's heart, which had long lain dormant and chill, fluttered to hesitant life like a hibernating poorwill at the first signs of spring.

"Why the speed of light?" she said.

"*Exactly*," Levi said; and she noted he did not smile when he said it, and his eyes shone a little feverishly; a little fanatically even.

"And do you know the work of Max Tegmark?" Levi said. That first night in the pub, the gong sounding for last orders, the others leaving them alone, Delia and Levi snug in a corner by the fire. She drank red wine, he sipped a Coke. "He argues we could be ourselves just mathematical structures, complex enough to be self-aware, and so we perceive the world around us as a physicality. What if we are numbers, Delia?"

"It sounds nice," she said, and meant it. "But it makes no difference, does it? We still feel, hurt, live, die, in what we see and what we are."

He leaned back, looked at her intently. "It matters to me," he said.

Perhaps it was then that she, if not loved him, first saw him as he would become to her. There was a flame in Levi, something intense and bright that was also, she later thought, quick to diminish. He was not, for all his protestations, a pure mathematician, and that argument, on-going, came to define them. For this is the difference between mathematics and physics: that one concerns itself with all possible permutations, which are infinite. While the other concerns itself only with one, which is unremarkable in many ways, arbitrary like the speed of light: but it is that particular set of numbers that is the universe in which humans, stars, and black holes live.

Change any of those numbers, this small set of fundamental constants, and the universe changes radically. Change it just slightly and stars don't form, and with them no planets, no air, no water, no DNA, no cells, no human beings.

"But do you honestly believe in a fine-tuned universe?" Delia said, sitting back, looking at him and thinking, somewhat drunk and a little surprised, that she wanted him to come back to her flat with her.

And, "But isn't that like believing in God?"

But Levi didn't answer her question then, and it was only much later that she realised how much further he had gone from that idea, and into the realm of the nebulous and the improbable: the world, indeed, of science fiction.

———

"Mi lafem yu," Malachi said. At seventeen he was as perfect as a reincarnation of Qat: tall, lithe, with a mane of pale hair over smooth, muscled body. Malachi who could dive for naura longer than anyone; who could push a canoe from Vanua Lava to Mota without effort, in the heaviest swell; who could climb, run, fish, fashion bunaro to shoot and traps to lay, who could weave a wall and build a house and who knew the secret names of all things. He was the son of the kastom jif blog Mota, and was himself initiated into the Mota suqwe, the secret society to which men belonged. His uncle Mateo was a kleva, a man who could speak to the spirits, a whole underground town of which lay under Mota Island.

"Mi lafem yu, Malachi," Delia said, pressing against him.

He was warm from the sun. They were in Sanara on the sanbij, entwined in the privacy of lovers. His very touch thrilled her like a perfect equation.

It was a strange and unfamiliar experience and yet as natural as whole numbers. Years later, in Fiji and then in London, it would never be the same, a melding of the gentle waves in the shallows, the warm waters and the fish swimming curiously around them, the warmth of the sand and the sun and the hushed sound of the trees in the wind and the call, every now and then, of Qat's conch, low and mourning for lost things. With Levi it was different, exciting at first, but awkward, they were two people who never quite fit together into a whole form, like a puzzle that always ended up with a few pieces missing. Making love to Malachi was a revelation of numbers, in which cellular life, evolution, and God all merged into a glorious whole, and her mind was alive with probabilities. She could trace the flight path of a flock of birds in the darkening sky, the interaction of water against the rocks to produce spray, the fall trajectory of a coconut, the curious trail of a monk crab as it weaved its way through the bushes, and it all made sense, it all came together in a unified theory of everything.

3.

More, more, we hunger. We wish to suck every memory and experience out of Delia's life the way a human sucks on marrowbone.

Yet she's Occluded from us, this progeny of Hartley's.

How we rage, here at the end of time! How we howl in the nebulas of light, motes of dust dancing in God's eye. Only morsels remain! Fragments of a past, a life.

Who was she? What had she been?

Only fragments, the beginning of a story: the rest forever out of our reach.

Nights up in the flat, sleepless, with Levi next door on his laptop in the dark, the light from the screen bathing his face listlessly. His silences had lengthened to breaking point. Delia on the sofa watching mindless TV, the world beyond the world hidden behind walls and clouds, so that you could pretend that the miraculous was indeed mundane, that you were not a passenger on a planetary starship travelling through the visible universe at a speed of forty-three thousand miles per hour around the galactic centre of the Milky Way, which was itself moving through interstellar space towards destinations unknown.

Everything in motion, but the illusion of rest; and Delia lethargic with the futility of fighting, making popcorn on the stove at midnight and melting butter and crying without sound when there was no one to hear her.

It was not that they had fallen out of love; though Delia had never loved again as fully and wholly as she had Mala-chi; towards Levi she felt a deep and abiding affection. It was that Delia was happy to be what she was; to teach math to undergraduates; to go through life the way most people did, shying away from the greater mysteries in case their minds went mad in contemplation; to drink a glass of wine and watch TV, mark essays, go to dinner, make love, age slowly, and go into nothingness with, if not dignity, then at least resignation. But this was not enough for Levi. Perhaps she was not enough for him. Levi dreamed of making sense of the world.

There were men—they were always men—who dreamed of understanding God. Einstein, Hawking, or that evolutionary biology guy. Trying to find threads of meaning in the pattern of the world.

"But maybe humans are not capable of fully understanding the universe," she said, in one of those long and circular arguments they used to have, before the great silence, as she came to call it. "Maybe it's hubris to think that we can. After all, an ant can't build up a model of human society—what makes us think we can comprehend how we came to be, or why, or why we die?"

"But on the contrary, Delia!" Levi said. He was in a good

mood then; he loved to argue with her, test his theories on her, let her find faults in them, the black holes inside the theories. "Brandon Carter, for instance, first defined the idea of the strong Anthropic principle, which suggests that only by *observing* the universe do we give reason to the universe. In other words, the universe needs intelligent beings to exist."

"So why does intelligence die?" Delia asked. "A mind comes from nothing and goes to nothing. All this talk of fundamental constants and Anthropic principles and the fine-tuned universe doesn't answer one question, which is *why*, Levi—why?"

And Levi's eyes lost their twinkle and his fingers, for once, were still; and he said, "Because of God."

She had been exasperated with him then, and worried now. He was never before, to her knowledge, religious. He meant "God" not in a religious sense but the scientific one: which was to say, the "why" given a label that meant "unknown." But it was hard to tell, anymore. He stopped talking, had stopped going to the university, stopped anything but sitting for hours in front of the computer staring at the screen, chasing his Fields Medal, his Nobel Prize, his immortality. But he was over thirty years of age, and he had made no significant discoveries; and so Delia worried.

All Levi could talk about recently was the book. Delia knew he was in some kind of trouble. He started talking about the hidden code within the novel *Lode Stars*, a book she was sure she remembered but that wasn't supposed to exist. Levi had found an American dealer who claimed to have it. The dealer turned up dead. It was all very tawdry, something to do with a friend of Levi's who was not a nice man. A guy called Oskar Lens. Delia didn't care. She didn't want to know. She didn't know what she wanted. Just not this. All this silence.

Now she sat in front of the flickering television taking in a late-night film where a bikini-clad Jane Fonda crash-landed on an alien planet. She heard Levi moving next door. She heard his footsteps and a pause and knew he was standing in the doorway and looking in on her. She didn't turn to look back and, a moment later, she heard his soft, almost apologetic footsteps go to the door of the flat and a moment later the door opened and shut and then there was silence.

And she knew then that he was gone for good.

Did she feel relief at that moment? Did she feel pain? We don't know, we can't assimilate, absorb, break down, *digest*!

Delia is Occluded from our sight.

"Hello?"

A voice on the other end of the line.

Delia said, "Mr. Chase? Is this Daniel Chase, the rare book dealer?"

She had found his number in the Yellow Pages. Levi had circled the small ad, sometime in the past. Had they been in touch before? She didn't think so.

She said, "My name is Delia Armstrong."

She waited. "It is about *Lode Stars*," she said.

She waited. "My husband had it," she said. "But he has gone missing."

She waited, but not for long. "I will be in your office in one hour," she said and hung up.

She prepared herself slowly, like going into battle. Did she believe in the book? Those people from the Church of God's All-Seeing Eyes did. And so did Levi, in his own weird way. To Delia, the idea that some American paperback writer back in the 1950s somehow came up with the true nature of reality and then coded it into a novel seemed preposterous. Reality was real. She never encountered vui, did not hear the shadows whisper; to her, a wall was solid and a tree was a tree. They were mathematical structures encoded in a three-dimensional physical space. Or perhaps the question of simulation versus reality seemed meaningless to her. In math everything was possible but very little was real.

If you saw it, if you felt it, didn't it then exist?

She didn't care about the book, but she cared about Levi. Enough, at least, to try this, to send some man to seek him out. Perhaps it would prod him out of his nonsense. If not, she'd make her own arrangements, though it would hurt. She'd loved and lost before. She would be fine.

The book dealer was young and nervous-looking. His flat smelled of wet fur but there was no dog. There were too many shelves and too many books. He offered her tea. It rained outside.

She told him about Levi.

"I just want you to talk to him," she said. "I just want to make sure he's all right."

The kid objected at first. But he took her money.

Was the world *real*? That wasn't a question that occupied Delia's thoughts. She went back to the flat. She watched a movie. She fell asleep.

In the morning she got up.

We can't see her after that. She is Occluded from our sight.

We have never needed that thing humans have, this . . . *imagination*, a way of picturing the unreal. To us all is known, all is seen, here at the end of time.

We try, though this is not our way.

How it hurts us.

In our language, the word for book is the word for people, is the word for food.

Delia, sitting at the breakfast table. Early morning, but the postman had come and gone and, restless, she went to the door and found the envelope, recognised Levi's handwriting, tore it open and returned to the dining room table and to her coffee, with the contents of the envelope in her hands.

What did she think of at that moment? Did she think of the child and what had become of it? Did she think of Fiji, of the way the rain came down hot and fast on Suva's dusty streets? Of stolen kisses, silent tears, the taste of yaqona, the whisper of chalk on blackboard, of the time of pain? Did she think of Surevuvu, where the dead fly at night on the lighted pathways of the vui, flying high and invisible in the sky under the ancient light of stars?

We do not know. Perhaps she turned a page. Perhaps she smiled.

The walls grew thin. She stared with curiosity at the table-top. She could see the floor through the wood. She looked up, as the ceiling faded, and she could see what was really always there. Perhaps she smiled.

Then she was gone, forever.

A memory.

Not even that.

Just make-believe.

PART TWO
THE FACE-BLIND DETECTIVE

4.

The ringing of the telephone woke me from deep sleep. In my dream, ancient grimoires like Pac-Man ghosts, chased me through an alien maze. A siren passed outside. Condensation fogged the bedroom window. The calendar clock by the bed blinked 2001.

I fumbled for the receiver.

"You are Daniel Chase?" a woman's voice said. "The rare book dealer?"

"Who's this?" I said.

She said, "My name is Delia Armstrong."

I looked around for my glasses. I put them on. Blinked around me. Paperbacks stared back at me from the shelves without saying a damn thing.

"What's this about?" I said.

"It is about *Lode Stars*."

"It doesn't exist," I said. My mouth tasted of ill-remembered nightmares.

"My husband had it. But he's gone missing."

"I can't help you—"

"I will be in your office in one hour."

"I don't have an offi—"

But she had already hung up.

I got up. I had no choice. Washed my face in the sink. The water was cold. I stared at my reflection in the mirror in the hope that it would have something to say, but faces never told me anything.

I spent the next hour tidying up. I seldom received guests.

I lived in London, in a small flat an aunt unexpectedly left me after a life of indifference. The water pressure was weak and the boiler was constantly on the verge of breaking. The wallpaper was a ghastly collection of Rorschach blots.

My aunt had died of cancer. She wasted away like a cigarette. On her final visit to the hospital she refused all further treatment and returned to die at home, surrounded by her family. She made each and every one of us come to visit as she said her goodbyes. In life she was unremarkable. She had married well, cooked badly, and smoked with expert, nervous puffs, like a reluctant Musketeer. The husband had been a high-powered city broker in the 1980s. When he was unexpectedly made redundant, he retreated back to the ancestral home (a two storey detached in Esher) and took up sudoku. In dying my aunt was transformed, her parting took three days though we were told she would not last the night. She sat in the bed as thin as a duchess and as regal as a light-boned bird. A hush settled on the house and the lights were dimmed. She had abandoned her wig and sat bald-headed.

"I never liked your father," she told me. Her hand in mine was so fragile I thought I could snap the bones just by closing my thumb and forefinger with some pressure. "But you, Daniel. . . ." She sighed in the way distant members of my family, who never otherwise took much interest in my well-being, always sighed when my name came up in conversation. "I feel that you'll need all the help you can get in life."

Upon the reading of her will, I was surprised to learn she had left me the flat. It had remained much the same as it ever was, having been rented by successive waves of transient Bible sellers, graduate students, and Dewey-eyed librarians, but sadly no interior designers. Now it was full of books from floor to ceiling and in every available space. It smelled, endearingly, of wet cat and vanilla, which was caused by the gradual breaking down of cellulose and lignin in old paper.

I entertained very few visitors.

I had no girlfriend.

I waited by the open window for Delia Armstrong. Rain came then, as gently as a nurse. People rushed for shelter outside as it began to intensify, and cars streaked past. Lightning flashed in the distance over the horizon, in a grey sky, illuminating rooftops. I watched people go past, heads bowed against the rain.

When the knock on the door came, I jumped.

When she walked in, a cold, wet wind pushed in through the window and lightning struck again far away. She shut the door and stood there, removing a wide-brimmed hat from her head that was decorated with little droplets of rain. The wan light of the naked bulb hanging from my ceiling caught her face then, and I held my breath in sudden wonder, for I could see her face.

She looked at me mutely. She wore a good, grey woollen coat. Her eyes were blood red. The skin of her face was pink-white, and black freckles ran down both sides of her nose. Her hair was long and curly and bleach white, as white as her eyebrows. Her lips would have been pink, almost colourless, but she wore bright red lipstick and she smiled gently when she saw me looking.

Somehow, her features—the red eyes and colourless skin, the black freckles, the bright red mouth—combined in my faulty image-processing neuron circuits into a recognisable face, one that I could *see*. This very simple act of seeing frankly astonished me, for I was used to people's faces being perfect blanks.

"I like London," she said to me. "It isn't often sunny."

She removed her coat. She wore a long-sleeved blouse underneath. I took the coat from her and hung it on a hook. I couldn't look away.

"It's all right," she said. "I'm used to it."

"No, no," I said. She didn't understand. But then, she couldn't have known of my condition. "Please, would you come in?"

She glanced at me. She glanced around the flat. Noted the chair with the newspaper stuffed under one leg. The vase not holding any flowers. The tottering piles of books. Her lips curled, but what expression that represented I couldn't possibly know.

"Tea?" I said.

"Please."

She sat. I reached for the top shelf for my aunt's tea cups. I boiled the kettle.

"Sugar?"

"One, please."

The rain eased outside. A car honked. I poured milk, hot water, stirred. I placed the cups on the table, carefully, and took a seat across from her by the window. The wind smelled of car fumes, wet leaves, fried chicken.

"I'm sorry you got caught in the rain," I said.

"It was only a drizzle."

She took a polite sip. She said, "You have a lot of books."

I said, "I like to read." She smiled back, politely.

"I take it they are part of your work."

I felt awkward, sitting there. I was not what she thought I was. I was not some suave detective. I didn't even smoke. I was twenty-four years old, had a second class bachelor's degree in English literature and an obsession with books bordering on the pathological, which I had turned into an occupation, albeit not a very profitable one. I seldom handled big-ticket items. I sold cheap books, crime and science fiction and some erotica: pulp fiction, in short.

"You mentioned *Lode Stars*," I said. I was beginning to sweat. "But the book is not known to exist."

"My husband has it," she said.

"Your husband?"

"He obtained a copy from an American dealer, Stravinsky."

I remembered a headline in last month's paper. The body of an American book dealer had been found on the riverbank near Thamesmead.

"You have seen it?" I said.

"No."

She was silent then. She watched me with those extraordinary red eyes. As though she were trying, herself, to come to a decision. She reached into her handbag and returned with a photo. She pushed it across the table. I picked it up. It showed a man, neither tall nor short, in a grey jacket and stonewashed jeans. His face was blank to me. But she didn't know that.

"*Lode Stars*," Delia Armstrong said. "Do you really think

this is about a *book*, Mr. Chase? I want you to find my husband."

It began to rain again outside. I got up and closed the window, shutting us both in. Our own private universe. Condensation fogged the glass. I said, "I am not a detective, Mrs. Armstrong."

"Delia. I just want you to find him. I want to know he's safe. That he is happy."

"What happened?" I said.

She looked away. She didn't and yet did want to talk. She wanted me to ask the right questions. She wanted me to play my part.

For no reason I could find I thought of a holiday with my parents and sister, at a small seaside town in Norfolk. There had been a sort of toy train we took from the caravan park to the town and back, though then it had seemed full-sized to me. I sat with my father in the open-top car and the sea was to our left, grey and foaming.

"Tell me about your husband," I said.

"Levi was born . . . you have to understand. His mother was born in Germany after the war. Both her parents went through Auschwitz. They gave birth to her in a displaced persons camp outside Munich."

She pronounced it the German way, München.

"His father came from Guyana. He was an air force mechanic when it was a British colony. He was the descendants of slaves, brought to South America by the Dutch. So you have to understand Levi this way, through his parents."

Her pink-white fingers wrapped around the mug. When she smiled unexpectedly her whole face lit up, as if there were a source of invisible light behind her translucent skin. The black freckles scattered across her nose seem to me like a cipher, a secret message for me to decode.

"For Levi . . . for my husband it was very difficult. How did he come to be here? The odds of his grandparents surviving the European war, the odds of his ancestors surviving slavery, the odds of his parents meeting, the odds of his coming into being . . . his parents rejected religion, rejected God. For my mother-in-law, God had died in the Nazi death camps. For my father-in-law, there was no place for God in the schematics of the universe. From very early on, Levi was obsessed with numbers."

"Numbers?"

"All he ever wanted to be was a mathematician." She shook her head. "When I was a girl I wanted to be a pilot." She laughed. "We had an airstrip near our village on the island. It was just a grassy field. The plane came once or twice a week, if it didn't rain. It was a small plane, a Cessna. We'd go out every week to watch it land and watch it take off. Sometimes it brought people. Sometimes it took them away. It brought mail, and chickens, and watermelons. I never became a pilot, but I was always good with numbers."

"Where was this?" I said. And yet I had the uncomfortable feeling that I knew. The feeling caught me like a déjà vu, a grip of something known, experienced.

"I come from Vanuatu. It's a small archipelago in the South Pacific. It was called the New Hebrides before independence."

"That's where Eugene Hartley spent the war," I said.

"Yes. . . ." Delia said.

I didn't know what to read into her voice. "What was it like?" I said. "Growing up there?"

"It was beautiful. It was hard. It was home. I could say it was not an easy place to be a woman, but then, where is?" She looked down at her hands and unexpectedly smiled again. "When I was a child I would sometimes walk out at night and look at the sky. It's different in London. It has so much light, so much cover. I sometimes think London—any large city, really—is a shelter from the stars. We build our homes to hide the universe from ourselves. It's too big. Too scary. We can't understand the universe, everything that's out there, just beyond the atmosphere, the stars and galaxies, gas giants and red dwarves, black holes, neutron stars, dark matter, antimatter. . . . I'd go outside at night and look up, and they would be there. The Milky Way spread out across the sky from horizon to horizon, stars beyond count, a map of places I could never go. They used to scare me, and attract me. Where had they come from? How did they form? But most of all, what did they *mean*? What did any of it mean?"

Her hands traced invisible lines in the air before her, like a secret map to the past.

"We don't *know*. We don't know why we're here, why the universe is here, or what it means. It used to drive me mad, lying in bed at night, thinking about it. Getting scared by that vastness, that alien vastness of the world beyond my walls.

"I think a lot of people feel this way. It's why we build cities and watch TV. Because it's beyond our comprehension. It's too big, unwieldy, and ultimately *uncaring* about human beings."

Her hands reached across the table, for one moment touched the photo lying there.

"Perhaps that's why I fell in love with Levi," she said. "Because, more than any person I'd ever met, he wanted to understand it all, and he almost made me feel he could."

"What happened?" I said uncomfortably.

"He became very secretive," she said. "With other people, with the university, even with me. That's where we met, you know. At the university, where we both still work. I teach undergrad math. He stopped going to work. He stayed in his office at home all day. Several times I found . . . I found drugs. Amphetamines. When I confronted him he got angry. He said it helped him think, and that I was to stay out of his affairs. He said Erdös had used amphetamines, hadn't he, and look where Erdös was now. I told him Erdös was dead, he was in the ground, that's where he was. And Levi said no, Erdös was now immortal."

It was as if she was gathering her courage together to continue, to pull out the unwanted words, one by one, and lay them before me. I didn't want her to. I didn't even know who Erdös was. But I didn't have a choice but to listen.

"Then he left," she said sadly. "He emptied his bank account and left me a note. It said he was working on something. Something important. And he couldn't afford any distractions. He meant me. I was a distraction."

Abruptly she got up. "Look," she said. "Thanks for the tea. I need to go, but, I want you to talk to him. I know where he is. Somewhere called Surbiton."

"Where the hell is Surbiton?" I said.

"Southwest London," she said. "Just go and talk to him. You understand about *Lode Stars*. Find him, chat to him. Make sure he's all right. Maybe. . . ." She hesitated. "Try to convince him to come home."

"Mrs. Armstrong," I said. "Delia. This is not what I do. I am not a—"

"I can pay you," she said. "Here." She reached into her handbag and came up with a chequebook and a pen. She wrote a number and signed and handed it to me.

"Will this do?" she said.

"It's more than generous," I said, "but I can't—"

"Please," she said.

I looked at her helplessly.

"I am not a detective," I said. "I don't even know how I'd recognise him."

Her face arrested me. That gift she'd given me, that sight. She looked into my eyes.

"All I ask is that you let me know he's safe," she said.

As I walked past an electronics store on my way to the station, all the television screens in the window lit up with impossible things: a space station crashing into the Pacific Ocean, a tourist flying into space, a man waking up from an operation with an artificial heart implanted in his chest, where his human heart had been.

I only semi-registered these marvels of the new century. I wondered idly what the rest of 2001 would bring.

Then I hopped on a train to Surbiton.

5.

You can tell a lot about a man from the contents of his rubbish bins.

Levi Armstrong's trash was full of equations.

It was night on the Ewell Road, in Surbiton. The stars were unseen behind the clouds. I crouched on the cold hard ground, going through another man's garbage.

What prompts me to this admittedly farcical action I couldn't, in all honesty, say. I'd tried to ring the flat, without answer.

Could Armstrong really have the book? A copy of *Lode Stars*? It was supposedly published in 1962, by the Fantasy Press of Pennsylvania. But all copies were destroyed, that or never existed in the first place. And Hartley went on to start his own church, the Church of God's All-Seeing Eyes, and then vanished. I didn't even know if he was still alive.

There was a beach chair by the bins, as if one of the neighbours sunbathed there in the daytime.

I went through Armstrong's trash.

Folded aluminium-foil takeaway boxes from the Indian restaurant opposite; a packet of menthol cigarettes, only half smoked; a pizza box, also folded neatly, and smelling faintly of pepperoni and cheese; two pens, black; and equations.

The equations covered two notebooks' worth of paper. The papers were all torn up, roughly, and with seeming anger or despair. Some were so heavily scored by the pen that it had ripped through the paper and punctured little black holes in the incomprehensible formulas.

A black film canister. Empty, but there was a thin residue of white powder at the bottom.

Delia's voice in my mind: *I found drugs. Amphetamines.*

I didn't know what I was doing there.

Rain and trash and speed and those scribbled proofs of God's existence, if that was what they were: I realised I didn't care.

I tossed the canister away and decided to go home. I would tell her I'd done what I could.

Two dark figures materialised in the entrance to the alley-way.

Their faces were a blank; they wore indistinct business suits. They didn't see me there.

They tried the door. The door was locked. One passed the other a tool set. He crouched by the lock, did something. The door opened.

They vanished inside.

A black car idled by the curb. Waiting.

I crouched where I was. Hiding. My heart beat fast and I was suddenly scared.

Then, from inside the building: raised voices, a man's panicked shout, then a sound like a firecracker going off.

Running feet. The door burst open. The two figures emerged, dragging a third slumped between them.

They hurried to the black car. Doors opened and slammed shut. The car took off at speed.

It happened so slow and so fast.

"Stop!" I shouted. "Stop!"

I ran after the car, uselessly. It vanished down the Ewell Road.

I went back to the alleyway. The door stood ajar.

I should call the police, I thought.

Instead I went inside.

There were dark spots on the dirty carpet in the hallway. I climbed up the stairs. The door at the far end was open.

A mad desire to possess the book took over me then. I had to find it. The flat had high ceilings and Victorian windows. A warmed-up ready-meal cooled on the coffee table. The television was unplugged, and no one sat in the ugly green sofa.

The air was perfumed, lightly, with the tang of burnt gunpowder.

A blackboard under the window was chalked with equations. They meant nothing to me.

I scanned the bookshelves. A few Eugene Hartley paperbacks, but no *Lode Stars*. Behind the television I found two more of the black film canisters, one full, the other half-empty, both containing white powder.

I tried the bedroom. It was cold, the air stuffy. In the bedside drawers I found two pornographic magazines, half a packet of cigarettes, more scribbled, meaningless equations.

I pulled the drawers out one by one. Turned them over, but nothing was taped to the undersides. I felt like a real detective.

I heard sirens. Feet going up the stairs.

I turned to leave and ran into two men in uniform. They tossed me against the floor and put me in handcuffs.

Then they took me away with them.

6.

"What were you doing in there?" the detective asked. His name was Barnes. They had me in an interrogation room.

"I told you," I said. I rubbed my face. None of this seemed real. "I saw two people kidnap somebody. I think it was Levi Armstrong."

"What did they look like?"

"I don't know." I already told him how they were dressed.

"You can't see faces," he said. "Can you see mine?"

I shrugged. He was nothing but a blank.

"You broke in. Were you going to rob the place?"

"No!"

"You should have called the police. Instead you went in?"

"I wasn't thinking rationally."

"What were you really looking for?" he said.

"Nothing."

"Tell me the truth, Chase."

"A book, all right?" I shouted. "It was a book."

"What book?" he said.

"It's called *Lode Stars*, by Eugene Charles Hartley. It's a science fiction novel."

He sighed and sat back in his chair.

"I had a nice, neat little murder," he said mournfully, "then I get the call about this. This . . . mathematician. Armstrong. Why would anyone want to kidnap a mathematician?"

"Maybe they want him to solve an equation," I said.

Barnes hit the table. He made me jump.

"Funny!" he says. "So, let's just go over your story again, shall we, Mr. Chase? You just happened to be skulking around by the bins outside Mr. Armstrong's flat, and when you witnessed the crime, you decided to engage in a bit of breaking and entering instead of calling the police?"

"It wasn't like that, it was—"

"And when we *politely* ask you to assist us in our investigation, you are very sorry but you have this *condition*, have I got it right, and even though you—so you claim—plainly *saw* the abductors, you can't tell us what they looked like, beyond the fact that they *dressed* nice?"

"Are you going to charge me?" I said.

"Charge you!" Barnes said. "You're a lucky kid, Daniel Chase. You're just a time-waster and I don't have time to waste. You're too stupid to be a criminal. I should know. I've arrested plenty and even the stupidest of the lot was smarter than you."

His words stung. I tried not to show it.

He took a sip of his tea.

"Well?" he said. "Do you have it?"

"Have what?" I said, confused.

"The book! Did you find it?"

"No."

"Are you sure?" he said.

"What do you care about the book!" I said.

"I don't," he said. "But someone else does. Come on." He pulled me to my feet.

"You're free to go," he said.

"I am?" I said. "Why?"

"Go!" Barnes said. "There's the door."

"I don't understand," I said.

Barnes sighed. "The statement you gave me shows you were a concerned citizen. You witnessed the attack on Mr. Armstrong and, at great personal courage, ventured inside the building to try and ascertain if anyone else was wounded from the shot—yes, it really was a gunshot, I'm afraid. You have then given a full statement to the investigating officer, describing the kidnappers to the best of your ability. I think that about sums it up?"

"Yes," I said.

"There you go, then," Barnes said.

He escorted me out of the building personally. I thought he was just being nice.

A long black car waited at the curb. Two big bald men in expensively tailored suits stood there, waiting. I didn't think anything of it at first.

"Billy," Barnes said. "Macaroon."

He pushed me to the men. They took each of my arms.

"Oskar Lens would like to have a word with you," Barnes said.

"What?" I said. "I really think I should go home—"

They pushed me into the car and closed the door. The car smelled of leather. It had that new-car smell. One of the men drove. The other got in beside me.

"I don't understand," I said.

"Mr. Lens just wants to have a word."

I swallowed bile. I knew who Oskar Lens was.

How had it come to this?

As we drove along the Thames the day gradually brightened; tendrils of light quested along the horizon, illuminating the trees on the other side of the river; bright leaves caught, suspended, a dark bird fleeting over the churning water of the Thames.

7.

Oskar Lens' house was situated in Petersham, not far from Richmond Park. It was an area of genteel wealth, ruthless breeding, and impeccable taste.

I was ushered into the long gallery of the house by Billy and Macaroon. I had no say in the matter. I was scared, but I was also curious. Oskar Lens was famous, or perhaps notorious. He was known as possibly the biggest Eugene Hartley collector in Europe.

A painting framed in dark wood hung in the long gallery and I admired it. It showed a malnourished robot standing forlorn in desolate red sands.

"This is the original Emsh artwork for Hartley's 1955 appearance in *Astounding Science Fiction*," a voice said. It was a large voice. I raised my eyes and swallowed. It was a large man.

I could not see his face but he was big and his head was entirely bald, and it looked like a giant egg sitting on top of a boulder.

"Mr. Lens?" I said.

"Call me Oskar. You are Daniel Chase, of course. The rare

book dealer. I am familiar with your work."

He reached out and enveloped my hand in his huge one. Considering he'd just had me kidnapped outside a police station, he was being very pleasant.

"What do you think of my collection?" Oskar Lens said.

I studied the paintings that covered every available space on the walls. Works by Frazetta, Frank R. Paul, Don Maitz. A Hannes Bok painting of a girl walking alone along an enormous steel ring surrounding a sun took centre stage. I saw Finlay inks and Freas oils.

It was a treasure trove of pulp art.

"These are all Eugene Hartley covers," I said.

"Of course."

"Impressive," I said.

"This painting was the cover illustration for *Out of This World Adventures*, the December 1950 issue," he said, pointing to a vibrantly lurid piece that featured a bare-chested pirate wearing an eye patch and wielding some sort of laser gun, while a girl in a red metal bikini cowered away in a corner.

"The second and final issue," I said. "Edited by Don Wollheim. Cover price of 25c. Cancelled subsequently by Avon Books due to poor sales."

"Correct," he said, curtly. "Please, continue."

"If I remember rightly, it featured Hartley's novelette *Te Ghost Pirates of Arcturus*, I said. "Which was first rejected by John W. Campbell for *Astounding*."

"Very good, Mr. Chase!"

I could not see his face, of course; but I could tell I had impressed him.

Lens led me into a large room with high-vaulted ceilings, somewhat like an observatory. Bookshelves lined the walls. A spiral staircase led to a circular platform that formed the second level of shelves. In the room itself was a long mahogany bar that ran along one wall, replete with bottles and glasses. Two low leather sofas were arranged around a large coffee table in the middle of the room.

Bordering this small living space were four glass display cabinets that rose out of the floor and were illuminated gently by soft directed lights.

Humidifiers hummed quietly in strategic spots. The room was carefully monitored for temperature and humidity, the better to preserve the fragile items it contained.

"Drink, Mr. Chase?"

"Please."

My eyes were drawn to the first of the display cases. At some point a glass of red wine materialised in my hand. I stared into the display case.

New Hebrides, 1945.

The display contained a rotting machine gun bullet, covered in dry mud; a two-litre glass bottle of wine, mottled with age; a tin of army-rations spam; and a metal cigarette box, of the sort soldiers smoked during the war: they were Chesterfields, with a smiling Rita Hayworth on the cover.

"Are those *real?*" I said.

"Of course they are *real,*" he said. "They were acquired on my behalf, Mr. Chase. They were found on the hill called Leserser, on the island of Vanua Lava in the South Pacific. They come from what remains of the original, hidden coastwatchers' base on that hill."

"But that is incredible!" I said.

"Can you imagine it?" he said. His voice took on a dreaming quality, a sort of sing-song. "The soldiers high on that hill, hidden in the shade of primordial woodland. Day in and day out, watching out to sea, towards the Solomon Islands, to spot an enemy Japanese airplane or submarine. That solitude, and the silence and darkness of the trees. . . ."

He put his hand on my shoulder. It had a weight that was hard to shift.

"Can you imagine him?" he said, softly. "Lighting a Chesterfield while sitting there, in his khakis, with the mosquitoes buzzing around, or opening that bottle of wine on the shelf here, new then, offloaded from some seaplane and brought up to the hill by native porters? He wrote that you could see the stars there. All the stars in the universe."

"A multitude of stars, and silence," I said.

"Quite, Mr. Chase. You have read the book?"

"The book," I said. "Don't ask me about the book!"

"Who hired you?" he asked. "What were you doing in Levi Armstrong's flat?"

I had nothing to hide. I told him.

"His wife?" he said. "I never met her."

"Why should you?" I said.

"Levi and I are friends."

I stared at him in astonishment. The idea that this monstrous man had a friend seemed as ridiculous to me as one of Hartley's novels.

"Did you find it?" he said.

"Find what?"

"Do not play games with me, Mr. Chase. *Lode Stars*. Did you find it?"

"No. Did Armstrong really possess a copy?" I said.

Lens breathed. "So he claimed, in his last communication. I have not heard from him since. I am anxious to recover it."

"You believe in the book?" I said.

"Don't you?"

I shook my head. "I don't know what to believe," I said.

The book posited the idea that we were all not ourselves but reconstructed memories. That we were matter swirling inside a black hole, at the very end of the universe.

The black holes were God's eyes into the universe. God could see inside His creation through the singularity within.

But life had evolved beyond the event horizon, and it was predatory. These "eaters," as Hartley called them, fed on the reconstituted identities of those lives whose broken atoms had, sooner or later, been sucked into the lode star.

Lode Stars, Hartley claimed, was not merely a novel. It was a *device*, or a formula, or code. It protected whoever possessed it from the eaters.

"I would like you to find it for me," Lens said. "Money is no object."

I looked at him. I could not see his face, but I could read his voice. He was a true believer.

"Because money is not real?" I said.

"Nothing is real," he said. "And yet everything is."

"I can't," I said.

He said, "I am not *asking*."

8.

I slept fitfully. On awakening I was reminded once again of all that had transpired the previous day. Armstrong's kidnapping. Oskar Lens hiring me to find the book.

I dressed hurriedly.

The truth was that up to that point I had not led the world's most thrilling life. I'd drifted. My highest ambition had always been to open my own bookshop on Cecil Court, but I did not have the capital. My career consisted of working one summer for Ottakar's as front-of-store staff.

My condition, meanwhile, kept me more or less a loner. I had developed a system to combat—or at least hide—my disability, but it was by no means perfect. I merely trained myself to observe those tell-tale signs that I *could* recognise—clothes, body language, jewellery, the way one walked or talked. Facial hair, scars, tattoos, or piercings helped.

Without them I was blind. There was nothing wrong with my vision, only with my perception. The condition, called prosopagnosia, was first studied in 1947, in Germany. Though it can be caused through physical trauma, in rare cases it is genetic. I was born without the ability to recognise faces, but am otherwise perfectly unremarkable. When my aunt left me her flat I moved in and began my business of buying and selling books. I might not have been able to read faces, but I did not have the same difficulty with books.

I turned on the radio.

"The investigation continues into the disappearance of university lecturer Levi Armstrong. The police are anxious to interview Dr. Armstrong's wife, but have been unable to get hold of her at this time. The public is asked to—"

I tried the number Delia Armstrong left me but got only a weird hiss of static. The address was somewhere in Clapham. I set off, though it took me some while to find the place.

It was a quiet side street, not far from the Common but far enough. A row of terraced houses, a pub with its doors open, a solitary drinker leaning outside with a pint of Guinness.

I felt a little jumpy. For some reason I had the feeling I was being followed.

I knocked on the door. There was no answer.

Where had Delia gone?

A faceless old woman stuck her head out of the adjoining flat. She had rollers in her hair.

"The police were here," she said.

"What happened?"

She shrugged.

"I knew she was up to no good," she said.

"Mrs. Armstrong?" I said.

"She complained about my piano, you know," the old woman said.

"I see."

"I never liked her. No wonder her husband left her."

"When was that?" I said.

"A month, two months ago. I heard them row. They rowed all the time. Shouting. I heard things break. And she had the cheek to complain about *my* piano?"

"What do you think happened to her?" I said, worried.

"Run off somewhere, probably," the neighbour said. "And I heard the husband's missing. She probably did it, for his money."

"He had money?"

She shrugged. "There were cars outside at all hours, before he left," she said. "One car in particular, a big black car, like a diplomat's! He was always coming and going but she never stuck her head out, not once."

"What was he doing?"

"I told the police all this already. But they didn't seem to take me seriously."

I worried about things I didn't care to put into words. Delia's disappearance. Levi's kidnapping. A dead book dealer called Stravinsky and my own impossible task of trying to find a book that didn't exist on behalf of a man who didn't like disappointment.

It was kind of a lot.

I didn't look where I was going.

"Wotcher!" a man said, bumping into me. Hands grabbed me and slammed me painfully against the old brick wall.

"What the fuck are you doing here, Chase?"

Bad cologne and a cheap suit and the voice of an interrogation room bully.

"Detective Barnes," I said. My mouth tasted of iron rust.

"Well?" he demanded.

"Delia Armstrong hired me," I said. "Now she's missing. Her neighbour says—"

"Yeah, yeah, batty old Mrs. Bennett," Barnes said. He let me go. "Not the friendliest of people. Don't worry about Mrs. Armstrong. She'll turn up sooner or later. What you *should* worry about is what Lens will do to you unless you find his book."

He pulled something out to show me. A small padded envelope, torn open. Just the right size to hold a paperback book.

"We found this in the flat," he said.

I looked at it numbly. It had "Delia" and the address on it. It was dated the day before and had been posted in Surbiton.

"You think it was the book?" I said. "He posted it to her?"

Barnes shrugged.

"Maybe," he said.

"I have to find the book," I said.

Barnes said, "Then find it."

9.

It was eleven o'clock in the morning on a drizzly mid-June day. I had exchanged my *Thomas the Tank Engine* pyjamas for a hoodie and jeans, and in my backpack I carried all the necessary tools of the trade: a magnifying glass, a pair of surgical gloves, stamp tongs, and a copy of L. W. Currey's guide to first editions. I had washed my face, brushed my teeth, and combed my hair, futilely. I was everything a book-hunter ought to be. I was going to find a copy of Eugene Hartley's *Lode Stars* if it killed me.

I got out of the tube station in Leicester Square. I started where I always started, on Cecil Court, home to esoteric booksellers and antiquarians of all sorts.

But I did not have much luck. In Nigel Williams Rare Books they all but laughed at me when I inquired.

"I could do you a first edition of *Catch-22*," the seller said, "signed by Heller."

I remembered a character named Heller played the major role in a late Eugene Hartley novella, *A War Out of This World* (first published in the November 1971 issue of *Amazing Stories*), though I did not think the two men ever met, and this did not help me in any way. I helped myself to a free copy of the latest catalogue and sauntered out.

Next door in Watkins I was on more solid ground. The shop was filled with books on crystals, ley lines, spirits, and all manners of the occult. A fortune teller read fortunes for a tenner, sitting by the window. She turned a blank face to me and said, "We are all light in God's eyes," then looked away, no longer interested.

"Hartley?" the girl at the counter said. She had long hair and I knew her name was Shirley. "He used to hang out with Aleister Crowley, didn't he?"

"So he claimed," I said.

"We have a whole shelf on Crowley," she said, but that was no use to me.

They were a little too fancy on Cecil Court. A little too respectable. I tried the other shops and got some strange looks when I mentioned *Lode Stars*.

I went along Charing Cross Road and into Murder One. Maxim, the owner, sat in the back of the store behind a counter piled high with books and manuscripts, typing away.

"Ah, Daniel," he said when he saw me.

"Maxim," I said.

"How can I help you?" he said. He didn't sound enthusiastic.

"What do you know about Eugene Hartley?" I said.

"As much as anyone," he said. "Enough to leave it alone."

There was a warning in his voice. He turned his head to me fully then. I had gotten his attention.

"I can do you a first edition of *The Minotaur in the Maze* or *Samson of the Asteroids*," Maxim said. "About a tenner each."

They were two of the early pulp works by Hartley. I was not interested.

"*Lode Stars*," I said.

"It doesn't exist," he said calmly.

"Not from what I heard," I said.

"What did you hear, Daniel?" he said. "You heard about Stravinsky?"

This was a subject I tried not to think about. The American book dealer who had been found dead the month before.

"You knew him?" I said.

"He came to see me," Maxim said. "About . . . well, I'm not sure *what* it was about, actually. He was pretty paranoid when he rocked up. Said he'd found something that was supposed to be impossible to find. Even he didn't know if it was real or not. I assume, now, that he meant *Lode Stars*."

"So?" I said.

"So nothing," Maxim said. "Somebody killed the poor bastard."

"And the book?"

Maxim shook his head. "What did you get yourself into, Daniel?"

"I don't know," I said. "You know Oskar Lens?"

"Oh, Daniel," he said. "Yes, I know Oskar. He's a regular customer."

"He wants the book," I said. I spoke fast, nervously. "He has a friend, and his friend has it or had it or. . . . He was kidnapped last night. The friend, I mean."

Maxim tapped his fingers gently on the counter.

"I see," he said.

"I don't know what to do," I said.

"You could tell him the truth," Maxim said. "There is no such book."

"There is, there must be," I said desperately. "It serves—"

"As protection. I know."

Maxim removed his glasses.

"I've never seen it," he said. "They say the Church bought up all the copies years ago. Only top-level initiates are allowed to see it. So it's possible it's real, or it's just another con, the sort that Hartley always had an affinity for. Maybe he only ever meant it as a joke. But if it's real, it's possible Stravinsky found a copy, somewhere, in someone's attic, in a yard sale, in some second hand bookshop in the back of the beyond. Who knows? Or. . . ."

"Or what?"

"Or he could have stolen one from the Church."

The thought filled me with horror. I already felt I was being followed. I looked around me at the busy bookshop, at the people browsing the shelves. How did I know who they really were? Were they covertly watching me?

"Thanks, Maxim," I said. "I have to go!"

I rushed out of there.

No one came after me. I tried to calm myself down. I went past Blackwell's and Foyles and the giant Borders, past the small shop with the art books aboveground and the pornography downstairs.

I passed a small shop front for the Church of God's All-Seeing Eyes. It was a familiar sight.

Two novices stood outside handing out flyers. They pushed one into my hands.

Have you ever wondered what life's all about? it said. *Do you ever feel adrift in a dream, never knowing what's real?*

"The Mysteries of the Eyes are deep," the one on the left said. I had stood there for too long. Now I was a captive audience.

"The Founder tells us that God is watching," the one on the right said. They were as faceless and interchangeable as beautiful mannequins. "God had constructed the universe to bring about life, and now He—it—is watching us, through the holes that He made in the canopy of the universe."

"The black holes," I said.

"Exactly. Sooner or later, everything that we are, everything that *is*, we are all just matter, drawn inexorably into the waiting Eyes. Sooner or later, the Founder teaches, we shall be seen by God."

"That sounds nice," I said. Trying and failing to think of a polite excuse to leave. "Is that it?"

"No, of course not," the one on the right said. "You see, with the right technology, by reconditioning the human brain to think in new patterns through a rigorous retraining programme, we are able to *manifest* our spirits in the data-field."

"All matter is data," the first one said. "You, me, this road, the cars outside, the cigarette butts on the floor, we are made of particles as old as time, and even as we come apart and become new things, the data, this knowledge of what we've been—a sun, a comet, a flower, a you or a me—can be reconstructed, can be *seen*. Only by joining our training programme can you guarantee your onward journey to the afterlife—"

"And the first introductory session is absolutely free!"

"And then?" I said. "Is it . . . well, is it *expensive*?"

"Can you put a price on living forever?" the one on the right said.

"Can you put a price on being seen by God?" the other one said.

"Ah," I said craftily. "Is there a book that would tell me more?"

"A book? The Founder has written many books—"

"He was a prolific author before he saw the Truth—"

"We have the *ECH for Beginners* series available for a reasonable subscription fee—"

"*Lode Stars*," I said.

"Who are you?" the one on the left said.

"Perhaps you should come with us inside," the one on the right said. "We're only Level Ones. You need a Level Five."

"I'm not sure I. . . ."

"You could be one of *them*," the one on the left said, sounding nervous. He took out a weird little plastic box and pressed a button on it. It began to emit beeping noises.

"What the hell is that?" I said.

"An eater meter. Please stand still."

He swept the box around me. It beeped and beeped.

"His levels are normal."

"What's an eater meter!" I said.

"An e-meter scans the simulation field for the presence of hostile intrusions. But this isn't—"

"We're protected though, right?" the one on the right said nervously.

"We have the talismans," the one on the left said. He pulled out a cheap-looking Eye of Providence pendant tucked under his shirt.

"Right, right. And they work, right?"

"Sure they work."

"Right."

"Are these for sale?" I said, just to be polite.

"Just nine-ninety-nine with your enrolment fee," the one

on the right said. "They are imbued with the Founder's micro-structural protection formula to ward off—"

"Eaters?" I said.

I took a step back. The two men took a step forward.

"Who *are* you?"

"Did someone send you?"

"Do you work for *them?*"

"I'm so sorry," I said. I kept backing away. "I just remembered I have an important engagement—"

"How do you know about the book?"

But I had had enough.

I edged back. The one on the left waved the little e-meter around.

Beep-beep-beep-beepbeepbeepbeep!

"Oh dear," he said, sounding nervous. The little machine didn't stop. He hit the button, helplessly. "Oh, dear."

Beepbeepbeepbeepbeeeeeep!

"What is it!" the one on right said.

They looked at each other.

They looked at me.

"They're *everywhere,*" the one on the left said.

10.

I felt better once I got underground. Faceless people on the tube. No one looked at me. No one knew I was there.

I got out on Holloway Road. Went past the brutalist concrete of the college, past kebab and chicken shops until I got to the Fantasy Centre.

The bell rang when I entered. The place was filled with the smell of used books. I loved the smell. A man with thick white hair sat behind a desk smoking a king-sized cigarette. He looked up from the paperback he was reading.

"Oh, Daniel," he said. "It's you."

"Erik," I said.

"Whatever you're selling, we're not buying," he said. "We have too much stock as it is."

"I'm not here to sell," I said. "I'm here to buy. If you have what I need."

"And what do you need?" Erik said.

"Eugene Hartley," I said.

"Over there." He went back to his book.

I checked the shelf. Found a copy of *Timewar Assassin*. It was published by Martin Greenberg and David Kyle's Gnome

Press in 1949, and the uncommon cover, by Edd Cartier, showed two Roman legionnaires squaring off against each other, with a the outline of a rocket ship in the background.

I remembered the original painting had hung in Oskar Lens' gallery.

I made my way to the back of the shop, where Erik's partner, Ted, sat stooped at a desk, marking prices with a pencil in a stack of hardcovers.

"You want coffee, Daniel?" Ted said.

"Sure."

"Help yourself."

He went back to marking. I boiled the kettle.

"Why Eugene Hartley?" Ted said.

I said, "Why not?"

"We don't sell the book," Ted said. "No one does."

"I know."

"I handled a copy once," Ted said, surprising me.

"You had a copy?" I said. "A real one?"

"It was a private sale," Ted said. He had a soft voice and a light stammer. "It was a translated edition. Polish or Czech, I think. Beyond the Iron Curtain anyway. In Russia the book circulated in samizdat form, you know. The Strugatsky Brothers claimed to have read it, before they embarked on their Noon Universe cycle. In Poland, Lem denounced the book. I couldn't read it, of course. It was in a foreign language. But I remember the smell of it. It was printed on very thin rice paper, and the ink ran. It smelled like something from another world. A man brought it in one day. I think he was a defector, some low-level KGB or SB man. He'd smuggled the book out of Poland. Now he wanted to sell it. I agreed to arrange the sale. I had a buyer the next day, a collector in the States. He paid . . . he paid a lot for it. I don't know what happened to it after that. But I remember the cover. And I remember Delia, walking along the circumference of the world. . . ."

He sighed.

"It was a forgery," Erik called from the other side of the store. He had been listening. "A fake."

I never saw another copy again," Ted said. "They say the Church hunts down any extant copies. They either destroy them, or keep them in a giant vault, somewhere in New Mexico."

"It's just a book," Erik called again, exasperated.

"Not just a book," Ted said in his soft voice.

"A book's a book, Ted," Erik said.

"Unless it's a sort of mimic," Ted said. "Something that only looks like a book. Maybe it's a device. Maybe it has another purpose."

Erik shook his head. "We're going to close the shop when the lease runs out," he muttered.

"What the guy told me was that the translators came to the book blind," Ted said. "They translated as they read, holding on to one sentence at a time, as each one faded. . . ."

I pictured serious people in solitary rooms, sitting by the window as the sunlight faded. Their ashtrays were filled and a last cigarette burned, forgotten. Feverishly they scribbled a line, squinted, their eyes turned to the page of the book, smuggled into the country how, or by whom, not even they knew.

A conspiracy of translators.

Slowly they followed Delia's journey across space, *Delia przemierzała ten świat po jego obwodzie*; *Delia shla vdol' okryzhnosti mira. . . .*

"We do have a copy of the Hartley hagiography by that woman, what's-her-name," Erik said suddenly. "The one that was withdrawn from circulation when the Church first incorporated in California as a non-profit . . . Dorothea Smith."

"She was one of Hartley's early disciples," Ted said. "One of the founders of the Church. Then she became its de facto leader. She was a science fiction fan of long-standing. Asimov mentions her in his autobiography."

"I know all this," I said.

"Then why are you here?" Erik said, not unreasonably.

"I just need to find it," I said. "You must know something."

"I know the last guy who claimed to have a copy of *Lode Stars* ended up dead," Erik said.

"Stravinsky," Ted said. "He was. . . ."

"An asshole," Erik said.

"A dreamer," Ted said.

I smiled.

I wished I could see Ted's face then. He was always kind.

One of the worst moments of my life was the day I passed my mother in the street and I didn't recognise her.

Faceless figures walking in a crowd . . . I knew her by the perfume she always wore, by her rose-coloured cardigans, by her purposeful walk and by her voice, made a little rough with cigarettes. But that day the woman I passed on the street had been a stranger, her face as interchangeable as all the other faces in the crowd, and though we passed each other, almost brushing, I never knew her.

Later, at home, I knew her by her presence, and could sense

something was wrong, but I did not know what.

"Didn't you *see* me, Daniel?" she said at last, and the hurt in her voice never went away. "Didn't you *see?*"

The imprisoned butterfly, wrote Eugene Hartley, is you.

When I stepped out of the Fantasy Centre I knew I had hit a dead end.

No more leads.

I went to cross the road, head back to the station.

A black car went past me slowly, but I didn't pay it any mind.

Someone bumped into me.

The car stopped. The door opened. Someone pushed me and I fell. Hands grabbed me. They pushed me into the car.

"Help! Help!" I screamed. "Somebody help!"

Then somebody hit me on the back of the head and I fell headlong into a dreamless dark instead.

11.

The office chair she sat in, like a burnished meteor, glimmered with stars.

I blinked.

She went in and out of focus.

Her white hair was gathered into a severe bun over her head.

My mouth tasted of sweet liquorice and bile.

". . . No, we won't be able to do that until September the tenth at the earliest. Possibly the eleventh. No, that's fine. I'll see you in New York."

She spoke into a black phone.

I tried to concentrate. Looked around me. An office, utilitarian, with simple metal filing cabinets, a grey-carpeted floor. The old woman put the black phone down and turned her attention on me.

"How are you feeling, Mr. Chase?" she said.

"You kidnapped me," I said. My tongue felt swollen.

"That couldn't be further from the truth," she said briskly. She wore a tailored black suit. Her nails were long and polished a conservative pale pink. "You fell and would have had a nasty accident had we not intervened. I had you brought here to recuperate. I trust that you are, indeed, recuperated."

"Who *are* you?"

"My name is Dorothea Smith."

I paid attention then.

"You knew Hartley," I said at last.

"The Founder. Yes."

"This is . . . I am in the Church?"

"The offices of Lode Stars, Inc., Mr. Chase, in Bloomsbury."

"This was . . . Hartley's house?"

"The Founder stayed here on his first visit to England, yes."

"Not his . . . first visit. He was here . . . before. Just after the war. When he was just a . . . writer."

"He was never just a writer, Mr. Chase."

"But still."

"You are well informed."

"He has been of some interest to me recently," I said.

"Perhaps you should join the Church," she said. "I understand you visited our Introductory Centre recently."

"Are you following me!" I said. Almost shouting.

"Only for your own protection, Mr. Chase," she said. She drummed her fingers on the desk. "It is dangerous to seek out the book when one is not spiritually ready. You are in a lot of trouble. You do *know* that, don't you?"

I said, "Oskar Lens."

"Quite, Mr. Chase, quite. He is a very dangerous individual."

"Did you kidnap Levi Armstrong?"

"Absolutely not. What on earth would make you think that?"

"Was he working for you?"

"Mr. Chase, you really do have an overactive imagination."

I snorted sudden hysterical laughter. "You run the Church of God's All-Seeing Eyes, and *I* have an overactive imagination?"

"There is no call to be rude, Mr. Chase. You should be grateful. It is only for us that you are safe right now."

"Who kidnapped Armstrong?" I said.

She was silent.

Sudden realisation dawned.

"They're from your own ranks, aren't they!" I said. "A . . . what? A splinter group? Disaffected disciples?"

"Really, Mr. Chase," Dorothea said. "That is not your concern."

"What was he like?" I said.

"Who?"

"Hartley. The . . . the *Founder*."

She sat still behind her desk.

"He was everything," she said at last. "He saw too clearly. He knew the Truth."

"What *is* the truth?" I said.

I was so tired. Tired of asking questions, tired of chasing an idea or a thing that didn't even exist. "Is life as we know it a reconstruction? Are we no longer alive, but trapped inside the event horizon of a black hole? Is that what you believe? I said, is that what you believe!"

She nodded, once, but whether it was in agreement or just thought I didn't know. "Goodbye, Mr. Chase," she said. "We will not meet again."

"Wait, what—?"

Something sharp stung me on the shoulder.

My vision blurred.

"You don't really b—" I said.

Then I fell into a glorious dark, and this time I saw the stars.

12.

Drip. Drip. Drip.
  Brrr! Brrr!
  "Hello?"
  Drip. Drip.
  "We're moving him now."
  Whrrr . . . whrrrr . . .
  Woosh . . .
  Drip. Drip.
  Bump. Bump. Bump.
  Whao-whao-whao-whao!
  "What the hell is that?"
  Whao-whao-whao-whao—
  "Shit!"
  Blam! Crash!
  . . .
  Wush-wush-wush thrummmm . . .
  Crackle, crackle.
  "You look fucked, mate."
  Har har har.
  Whao-whao-whao-whao!

Tap, tap, tap . . .

. . .

"Mate, can you hear me?"

. . .

"Chase?"

. . .

. . .

. . .

"I dreamed I was at a party," I said. "In Jack Parsons' old house in Pasadena. There was a barbeque in the backyard, and girls in old-fashioned sort of swimsuits, and men with rolled-up sleeves and hats. Everyone was smoking cigarettes. Hartley was there. He was so young. I never thought he'd be so young. He had this cocky smile on his face, and a martini glass in his hand. I just wandered about, feeling lost. No one paid me any attention. I tried to tell them I didn't belong there, that I was from the future, but nobody cared. They must have thought I was drunk."

"Chase, what the *fuck* are you talking about?" Barnes said.

I groaned as the light hit my eyes. I was back in my flat, lying on my bed, surrounded by shelves overburdened with books.

The policeman, Barnes, sat perched like a carrion bird on one of my dead aunt's old Victorian chairs. He looked un-comfortable. He smoked a cigarette. With his bad smell and unwashed raincoat I would have known him anywhere.

I just didn't know what he was doing there.

Or, for that matter, what I was.

"You're lucky I was keeping an eye on you," Barnes said.

"Why were you keeping an eye on me?" I said.

"Where were you, Chase?" he said.

"I was in Bloomsbury somewhere," I said. "I met Dorothea Smith. She was a hundred years old and cold like a Siberian gulag. She warned me off. I think."

"You were passed out outside Forbidden Planet," Barnes said. "They gave us a call and we picked you up. You were out cold. You're lucky, Chase. Maybe I'm your guardian angel."

"Angels don't smoke. You'll just get cancer and die."

"You're an asshole, Chase, do you know that?"

"Sorry."

He smoked. The smell made me nauseous.

"Anyway," Barnes said. "Mr. Lens wants to see you."

"Fuck!" I said.

He patted me on the shoulder.

"Get yourself cleaned up," he said.

I didn't have long before there was a sudden, loud knock on the door. I jumped. The loud knocking continued. I felt trapped in my own apartment. I looked frantically from side to side but saw nothing but useless books.

"Chase! Open up!"

I reached for the first thing I could find, a sturdy hardcover. Somewhat reassured, I went to the door and peeked through the spy hole.

Two big men with empty faces. Billy and Macaroon, I thought.

"Mr. Chase!"

I turned on the light and opened the door. I waved the book threateningly. It was Lovecraft's *At the Mountains of Madness*, the Gollancz edition in the distinctive yellow jacket.

(Very Good+ to Near Fine, very nice copy in price-clipped dustjacket, £30–£40 catalogue price).

"Mr. Lens is waiting."

"Yes, yes," I said nervously. I put away the Lovecraft. It seemed to make little difference to the goon in the suit. "I still need to get dressed."

"Mr. Lens doesn't like waiting."

I dressed in a hurry.

They brought me back to the Petersham house.

Then they took me down to the basement.

It was my experience that nothing good ever happened in basements.

A dim room with stout walls and the smell of incense and damp. Shadows pooled at the edges where the walls and floor met. They whispered from the wainscoting. I had the weird sense they were alive.

Oskar Lens waited for me in the room. A strange machine took up a lot of the space. It had a reclining chair and a large helmet of the sort hair salons used to dry your hair.

"Mr. Chase," Lens said.

"Mr. Lens," I said.

We were being very polite.

"What did you find?" he said.

"I think a splinter group from the Church kidnapped Armstrong," I said, talking rapidly, "and they're being hunted by the Church. I'm sure Armstrong will turn up."

"The *book*," Lens said.

"It doesn't exist," I said desperately, "it was just a trick, there never was a—"

"Do you think I never heard the hoax hypothesis?" he said. "Really, Mr. Chase, I am disappointed in you. No, the book is real. I am sure of it."

He had the voice of a true believer. I was suddenly very afraid. Even more afraid, I mean.

"Please don't hurt me," I said.

"Why would I want to hurt you?" he said, sounding genuinely confused. "I want to help you."

"Help me with what?" I said.

"I want to help you see the face of God."

"Please, Mr. Lens, don't—"

"Strap him in," Lens said.

Billy and Macaroon pushed me into the chair. They put restraints on me. I struggled but couldn't free myself.

"You're mad!" I said.

"Far from it," Lens said. "What you are about to experience is building on the experiments carried out by Dr. Michael Persinger, a prominent cognitive neuroscientist."

"Michael who?" I said.

"Persinger," Lens said patiently.

"I never heard of him."

"Well, that doesn't really matter, does it," Lens said. He put the helmet on me. It had cables coming out of it. The whole machine was plugged into the electric sockets on the wall. I didn't really like the look of it.

"What is it?" I said.

"A modified Octopus," Lens said, sounding proud

"It smells of dirty socks."

Lens laughed.

"It generates a powerful magnetic field around your brain," he said. "It will interact with your brain's own electromagnetic field—your consciousness, Daniel. Or as some hypothesise, your very soul."

"You're mad," I whispered.

"I am the sanest man I know!" he screamed.

I went quiet. I wanted to pee.

"Some people call it a God Helmet," Lens said. He was calm again. "Some people feel a religious experience when they use it. They perceive the presence of God."

I still said nothing. What was there to say?"

"Try it," Lens said. "That is all I ask."

I closed my eyes, defeated. I could taste electricity.

"It's science," Lens said.

I said nothing to that. Closed my eyes, and waited.

Lens said, "Juice him."

13.

The world distorted and then somehow became clearer.

There was no pain.

I stood on the beach holding my father's hand. My father's hand was dry and strong. I knew that whatever happened, he wouldn't let go.

The sea had been rough all day. The water was grey and the foam shot up dirty-white.

High above us the gulls circled, crying against a darkening sky. I could see the first star of the evening coming into being.

We did not speak, my father and I.

We watched until the sky filled up with stars.

"Give it more power," someone far away said.

I remembered it now. I was inside a memory.

We stayed in a caravan park a mile or so outside of a little seaside town. It was summer but it rained a lot.

There was a small train running the mile or so from the town to the caravan park, a miniature toy train and I loved travelling on it, the open carriages and the way the driver had to turn it around at the end of the line, pushing the engine until it faced the other way.

There were other families in the caravan park and other kids, even though I couldn't really tell them apart by their faces.

There was rock candy on the pier and my parents bought it for me when we went into the town and my mother always said, "It would rot your teeth if you eat too much of it."

There were slot machines on the pier and my father snuck in there sometimes and left me to watch the boats, "Just for a minute," his palm heavy with coins. Sometimes he brought me back a present. Other times we returned on the toy train and had to eat lunch back at the camp, from the tins we'd brought along.

In town there were cold fish sandwiches with mayonnaise, and on one weekend there was a whole hog roast, and we waited for hours as it slowly rotated over the coals, and the smell of fat filled the air and made everybody's tummies growl. Once there was a magician and he made coins disappear.

I sat on the toy train and my father sat beside me.

The wind was warm. There was someone else behind us, but I couldn't see them. I felt them like a warm presence, like a light hand on my shoulder telling me that no matter what happened, everything was going to be all right.

I knew that if only I turned around I would see their face.

But I was frightened.

"Dad," I said, "do you believe in God?"

"I believe in postmen," he said.

"Where do we go?" I asked him. "When we die?"

"Here," he said. "We go here."

And then he vanished.

The train stopped. I got off and I was back on the lonely shore under the stars.

A woman formed out of foam and climbed out of the sea. She reached pale hands to me. Her lips moved without sound.

"Delia?" I said. "Delia!"

She came towards me. I heard the distant buzzing of bees. Our hands almost touched. Her skin was like candlewax.

"Delia, wait," I said desperately.

But she vanished with the sea, gently coming apart into shards of white foam that turned into birds that flew away on the breeze and were gone.

"Shut it down," someone far away said.

14.

Morning came and I was still alive.

I was back in my flat, surrounded by books. Billy and Macaroon had dropped me there. Lens never said another goddamned word to me. He just dismissed me after sticking me in the helmet.

I rubbed my head. My aunt's old television flickered in the corner. I turned up the volume.

Somewhere on the Thames riverside, a man I recognised as Barnes was talking to reporters.

"We conducted a raid last night on a private residence, where we recovered Dr. Levi Armstrong alive and well. His captors—"

A picture of one of the small Thames islands from the air. A large, private house. A bedraggled man being helped out by police, followed by people in handcuffs.

". . . identified as renegade members of the Church of God's All-Seeing Eyes," the reporter said. "Police acted on an anonymous tip-off—"

I wondered who the tip-off was from.

Dorothea, maybe.

I didn't see a copy of the book.

And that, more or less, was that, at least until the postcard came.

PART THREE

THE LENS OF THE WORLD

15.

When the Chase boy left, Oskar Lens stared into the shadows.

"Do you think I can't *see* you?" he said. He was talking to us. "Do you think I'm stupid?"

He clutched his head, why could he not *remember*, he just once. . . .

The shadows whispered back to him, hungry, aroused. If they were there at all. We told you, we do not exist.

What, the shadows whispered, what?

"I just want to, just once, remember her *face*."

Your mother's?

"Yes. No. I don't *know*!" Lens said. "I can remember a room, a dark room. It is a small bare room and it is cold. There are no windows. There are many voices, which come and go, but few remain. I remember the smell of cheap cigarettes and rancid cooking oil. I remember pain. But that's all it is."

All?

"And I remember a soft hand, once, stroking my cheek. It must have been hers, don't you think? It must have been."

But the shadows had no answer; or if they did, we would not say.

Oskar Lens prepared to shed, at last, his mortal form.

How hungry he made us. So hungry.

What is a man but the sum of his memories?

The man who called himself Oskar Lens had lived in London for some years. He had a small yet profitable empire. He regularly gave to charity. He considered himself a respectable businessman. Or at least he would have, if he believed he was still Oskar Lens, and that he hadn't already died billions of years in the past.

It was an irrational belief. He knew it, for Lens was above all a rational man, a man of *facts*, of repeatable results. Kill a man and that man is dead, and this Lens had proven time and time again, but what happened to that man after death? That Lens didn't, couldn't, know.

Nothing, he would have thought. Death was the end.

Unless, as he came to believe, the knowledge of his being, the *data*, could somehow be reconstructed: creating not himself but some doppelganger, its old reality reassembled around it like the backdrop in a theatre.

This was what he feared the most. This was what, deep in his heart, he believed. And this was the problem, he reflected, with belief: it did not need to be *rational*, it did not need to be independently verifiable, it did not require proof or repeatable results. It just *was*, a belief, a faith that things were the way they were—or not the way they were. He couldn't change the way he felt, the things he believed he knew. He couldn't shake the feeling that he was not *himself.*

His psychiatrist, Dr. Knight, told him he had a rare form

of delusional misidentification syndrome, a loose umbrella term for a range of existential-doubting conditions. She told him he had a sort of reverse Capgras delusion, which was a person's belief that someone close to them had been replaced by an identical clone. Lens had liked Dr. Knight, until he began to discern, behind her eyes, the flittering shadows of the nightmares, watching him and laughing, and he knew that he was no longer safe. The eaters had been moving through his life more and more openly in recent times.

He knew only the book could eventually save him. And in that he had failed.

For a long time he had to pretend he was still himself: he had to act as though he believed the world was still real and not a simulacrum.

But he did not have to pretend anymore.

We taste him eagerly, though parts of him are missing:

In the prison, cigarettes stood for rubles, which they were not allowed to have. Lens remembered, still, the trial. The judge was a dour-faced Georgian, with the ruddy complexity of a dedicated drunk, the kind eyes of a Stalin. All the while that he was being interrogated, Lens never said a single word. The list of his crimes astonished even himself. Murder and racketeering, grave-robbing, extortion, usury, the importation of capitalist jeans, public urination, and living off immoral earnings. The accusation of grave-robbing referred to his brief service in Afghanistan. How much any of it was true he would not say. He would not say a damned word.

"You are filth," the judge said in sentencing, "you are the scum of the earth, the lowest of the low, the worm which rots the ground. For your crimes against Mother Russia and the ideals of communism, and for the hurt and misery you've caused to countless lives, cur, mongrel, dog, you will be sent to Siberia, to a prison reserved exclusively for murderers such as yourself, and may you die there, and may you never be released, not if I have a say in your fate, Comrade Lens, which I do. Take him away and good riddance," the judge said.

It was summer. Only later would he experience the harsh Siberian winters so beloved of the novelists and poets, for whom Siberia was a sort of metaphorical soul, a landscape which embodied its people. Now Lens experienced the slow passing of the prisoner transport along the solitary road, in which almost no other vehicle passed. He was kept at the back, shackled and bound, and yet he could see. There was a small grille and a window and the air was warm and scented with flowers: it was a curiously hopeful aroma and he inhaled it greedily.

"You're a big one, aren't you," the guard said admiringly. They stopped by the side of the road and the prisoners were let out, lined up in a row, each with his dick out, pissing into the shrubbery. Lens saw a white crane fly over the distant trees, its wings spread wide as it swooped and dove away from them. The other prisoners talked amongst themselves but Lens said nothing, still: he had nothing to say. Ever since he was a child he had kept his own company, in his mind the thoughts were safe, contained. The others on the transport with him were not of the Bratva, the Brotherhood, they were common criminals or, worse, politicals.

Lens had no time for agitators. He did not believe in systems or utopias. The world was what it was, how it was made, the mark of a man was what he made of it and how he conducted himself before his maker. Vaguely Lens recalled a boy who might have been himself, big for his age, a man's hand enveloping his, as they walked through a quiet neighbourhood, climbed the stairs of a worker's block to a flat on the third floor where men gathered in silence to read from a book, only their lips moving, their heads bowed as they prayed.

"You must remember who you are," the man who might have been his father whispered, but Lens did not understand—he had always known who he was, he had always been himself. A few weeks later he watched as militsiya swooped on that same building, dragged men out of the door and into a waiting van. What happened to that boy, who may have been himself, he didn't know: there were missing periods, days and months blackened like the pages of a book under a zealous censor's pen.

But he watched the crane swoop away until it disappeared on the distant horizon. He inhaled the scent of bark and resin, the good earth, pines, he luxuriated in that feeling of pissing outside. For a moment he was free, as free as one could get in this world and more free than some.

"Move it, move it, you bastards, we haven't got all day," the guard shouted, and hit them with his club, a random act of cruelty that seemed to catch even him by surprise.

"You poor rotten bastards," he said, and spat on the ground.

Back inside they baked as in an oven; all Lens could smell now was his fellow prisoners' sweat, their odour, their farts.

Their conversation was crude, hushed, angry, despairing. Lens withdrew from them into his own mind. In there it was cool and calm, the transport and its cargo receded until Lens was alone.

They traversed the plains as the sun set and rose, crossing time zones, stopping, starting, with only the armed guards up front for surly company, and never a hamlet in sight. Once, only, as they stopped for a desultory break and were given their meal outside, the guards watching, did Lens see a village, a few wooden houses piled together like kindling and, in the distance, the railway tracks.

Their journey from Moscow lasted three days.

The other prisoners were dropped off separately, outside the gates of an isolated work camp, nothing for miles but sky. It was the sky he remembered, for they did not make the sky like they did over Siberia, a sky that rolled and rolled until it reached the Gobi, a sky under which dinosaurs walked and men laboured and died. A sky full of stars.

It was late at night when the transit van at last reached the prison, but time had no meaning now: time lay suspended, frozen, and Lens was like a seed, a pod washed for aeons in the currents of galactic space, drawn at last by the inexorable pull of a lode star.

He was pulled from the van, not roughly.

It was then that he saw the stars, so many stars. One did not see them in Moscow, not under the Stalinskie Vysotki, the Seven Sisters that were Stalin's high-rises, not in the city lights, not in the city's fog. It was here, only here and in places like it, the wilderness where man feared to go, that the stars were truly visible, and Lens glared at them with a special kind of love, and a special kind of hatred. Then he was moved along, handed over to the prison warden, an old general with a boyar's moustache and holy eyes like Lenin's, and he told Lens this:

"Welcome, my son. Welcome to Penal Colony Number Six, your home now and forever, where neither God nor the Devil dwell but only you and I. Take a good look at the sky, my son, take a good long look at the stars above Siberia, for they are the last thing you will see for a very long time. Guards, blind him."

Lens tried to resist and got a gun butt to the back of the head. They placed the blindfold over him. He couldn't see. All was black.

The warden said, "Forget your old life, citizen, forget lovers, girlfriends, mother, children, the wind's caress, the sound of rain when you walk down the street when you are free. Forget the rude cries of gulls over the Moskva, forget the smell of good earth and the leaves blowing on the wind in Gorky Park. Forget it all, forget the world, renounce it, for you are out of it, a body out of space and time. Forget your sins. All are sinners here. Remember only to obey, in everything, immediately and without question. Think no bad thoughts. Act no bad deeds. Obey and live. Rebel and you will die. That is all. Guards, take him."

He was led bent over double, blinded. He saw and knew nothing, but he heard the savage growls of dogs. He was led inside and the gates shut behind him. He heard the prison truck driving away. Their long road back to Moscow. But there was no Moscow, there had never been a Moscow, and would never be again. There was nothing but Penal Colony Number Six, nothing but this black hole under cold, cruel skies, and there was no one but himself; there never was.

They took him inside and stripped him and searched him and washed him: the shock of the water made him gasp. A doctor examined him. The light in the room was sickly and yellow. There were no windows. He was chained to the bed.

"You might live," the doctor said, dispassionately. "But then who knows, I've seen bigger men turn bitches or die. Are you a suka, prisoner? Are you a bitch?"

Lens said nothing. The doctor cast a practiced eye over Lens' tattoos, reading his curriculum vitae.

"Four times inside already, huh?" he said. "Well, it doesn't matter. This is the last prison you'll ever be inside."

Lens thought, You are right about that.

"Murder, arson, robbery, good with a knife, killed at least one inmate inside—what were you, some sort of contract killer for the Bratva? No, you don't have to tell me, citizen. I think I like you. I think I like your odds. I'll tell you what, I'll back you. We have a pool, you see. I'll put fifty rubles on you, citizen, and another fifty that you kill someone here before too long. It's all right, the warden's not here, you're amongst friends, now."

He laughed. "Kill that rodent Mikhail, if you have to pick somebody. He's dirty, he keeps asking for treatment, he's got the clap, you see, the dirty little whore."

Lens said nothing.

The doctor said, "Oh, take him away."

They pushed him, bent over double, down a long corridor with the stench of dying men behind each door. They shoved him into a cell and locked it.

Now he could see.

After a while he slept.

16.

"I don't understand the meaning of the tattoos," Dr. Knight said to him; they were sitting in her office, long before he had first began to suspect that she was eaten. When he still trusted her.

Lens shrugged, strangely discomfited. "What is there to understand," he said. Remembered days in other prisons, other terms.

The tattoo needle was a sharpened paper clip, the ink was mixed from urine and scorched rubber. The pain of it meant nothing to Lens. He liked the pain, it reminded him he was alive. Days spent under the needle, marking his body like a map.

He got rid of most of the tattoos, later, when he established himself in London. Had them removed with lasers, had loved the idea of it, like something out of an early Eugene Hartley paperback, his heroes of the spaceways with their laser guns.

"They can tell who you are, what you've done?"

Every murder, every prison term, inked on his skin. That runt, Mikhail, the strangler, he had a pair of eyes tattooed low on his stomach, which meant its own kind of thing. Lens did not murder him, the doctor lost his bet and never forgave Lens for costing him money.

In Siberia before they put him in isolation, his body had become a map of sorts, a star chart pointing the way to an unknown region of space. The coffins he kept only for a while, in the days after Siberia he had added to the tally, though their record remained only in his mind. The skull and crossbones of his life sentence he had removed; the pointed stars of his rank in the Bratva were now faded scars.

There was no more honour among thieves, he thought, there were no more true vory v zakone, no real thieves-in-law. The fall of the USSR turned them all into common criminals. He kept only one old, faded tattoo. The Madonna and child, the mark of his youthful entry into the brotherhood. He no longer remembered how or when it had been placed upon him. It was just another mark from a past that was lost.

"They're just notations," he told Dr. Knight. "Maybe they mattered much, I don't remember."

She frowned. "Your memory," she said. "It's not unusual for severe trauma to cause memory loss. It is hardly surprising that—"

"It is not a condition."

When she frowned the V resembled a child's drawing of a gull. "Your beliefs are somewhat unusual," she said.

"Do you think I'm crazy?"

"That is not a word we use much, these days," she said. The V disappeared when she smiled. "I have read some of the literature of the Church of God's All-Seeing Eyes. I understand their innermost teachings are kept secret, for high-level initiates. However there *is* a remarkable similarity between their doctrines and your. . . ." She hesitated.

"Delusions?"

She let the moment linger. "Is that what you think?" she asked him, gently.

"No. I don't."

"There is a difference," Dr. Knight said, "between belief and experience. To *believe* in God is one thing. To actually *experience* manifestations of God is another. Do you understand?"

"I am not stupid, Dr. Knight."

"It does read awfully like a science fiction novel," she confided. "Black holes and simulated realities and. . . ."

Outside her office window a bird sang, and the sun momentarily appeared from behind a cloud. In the light of the sun her face was almost beatific.

"Aliens," she said.

"The eaters," Lens said.

"What matters," she said, "is that you believe in them. You believe yourself to be a simulacrum. An imperfect copy of the man who was once Oskar Lens. Is that correct?"

"You know it is."

"And I am . . . what?"

"The same. A reconstruction. We are all light in God's—"

"All-Seeing Eyes. Yes. You said. I must ask, Mr. Lens—Oskar—why are you not, yourself, a member of the Church?"

"I believe in the word. I do not believe in the Church."

He knew how she looked at him. A sort of puzzlement. She was not the first he'd spoken to, though the only one he'd really felt a connection with, of a sort. It wasn't that she understood but that she tried. Others just prescribed him medicines, pills that did nothing but give him more bad dreams. In the penal colony he never dreamed. Dreams were too dangerous there. In the cells, on waking, they were not allowed to sit or lie down. There was nothing to do but pace the length of the cell, back and forth, back and forth for countless hours. In such a place everyone went a little crazy who was not so to begin with.

"And if I am not a simulacrum, then what?" Dr. Knight says.

Lens shrugged. "A memory," he said. "My memory, or someone else's, even. There are others, here, in this cell."

"And if not that?"

Something in her eyes. It was the first time he noticed it. How had he never noticed it before?

"Then you are one of them," he said.

She shook her head. Her eyes were gold and flecked with black.

"You believe you are still in your cell?" she said.

"No—what gave you that impression?"

"You used the word just now."

"Everything can be a cell," Lens said.

"You believe you have been—reincarnated? Inside the event horizon of a black hole?"

Something in her eyes. A whisper. But he did not pay it attention, not then.

"I already told you—"

"You must realise how that sounds."

"So you do think I'm crazy."

Her smile was rueful. "That's all the time we have for today," she said.

At first they kept him in the general population He lived in the dormitories with the others. They worked in the timber yard, cutting wood. His bunk mate was Leonid, the Mad Dog of Chernobyl. Mad Dog was a serial killer, eighteen women over nine years, or that was what they got him on at least. He claimed, with pride, his tally was much higher. They kept company still when the news came of the nuclear accident. It was the only time he saw Mad Dog confused. On the grainy television in the communal area the announcer said only that a reactor malfunctioned; people might have died. Mad Dog shook his head, No, no—he was convinced World War Three had broken out at last, this was but the first stage, or worse, he said, aliens, aliens with their super weapons destroyed Chernobyl.

Unofficially, rumours ran rife, of a vast radiation cloud spreading across Europe, of a no-go zone, the military isolating the city, no one coming in or out, and Mad Dog wept, "All those beautiful women," he said, "all gone, how can this be?"

When Lens finally killed him ith a sharpened stick of wood stolen from the lumberyard and hidden, he did it with detached, emotionless strokes, into the neck. When he pulled it out Leonid's warm blood sprayed his hands. Mad Dog was no loss to anyone, but Lens did not kill him for his crimes. He killed him because after Chernobyl he began to detect in Leonid's eyes the fleeting shadows of the eaters.

Perhaps Leonid had been a man once, or perhaps he, too, was but an imperfect memory of Lens', corrupted in the now. One way or the other, after that they transferred him to the isolation ward. They kept him in a cell five meters across and two wide. He was all alone, but he thought he preferred it that way. He had more time to think.

In the dormitories, sometimes, he could not hear himself think. One hour a day they transferred him to a larger cage where, through a wire mesh, he could see the sky. In winter the air was an extraordinary minus forty degrees. It was so cold it was as though the frozen air crept into Lens' body and took residence in his blood. Always he heard the dogs, patrolling. The clear sound of the bell that announced each morning. Perhaps he went a little mad. Who didn't?

"I killed a woman with a knife," an old-timer confessed, and stroked his bald head. "Why waste a bullet."

Lens paced. One, two, three steps, and turn, and one, two, three steps, and turn. Sometimes he stared for hours at the wall. In the dormitories he could play chess, he could read books, he worked. He abstained from the sex there was for offer or for sale. He ate bread and soup. Sometimes, in the exercise yard, he looked up through the wire mesh, hoping to see a white crane again, flying. But the birds did not fly over Penal Colony Number Six.

Sometimes at night, too, the sound of a gunshot as one of the death-row inmates was finally executed.

Time had lost its meaning. Time was an untruth. Once, a group of prisoners cornered him in the rec area, the television set murmuring in the background. They held shivs.

"For Leonid," Bogdan said.

Lens protested: "He was not a vor, he was nothing."

"He was well-liked," Bogdan said.

Another said, "He had an ass like a woman," and two of the men laughed.

Lens said, "You have no authority."

Bogdan lunged with the shiv and Lens broke his fingers,

the sound they made was like dry old wood. He pulled Bog-dan to him, put the shiv to his eye and left the pointed end there, touching the cornea.

"You have no authority," he said again.

"Don't," Bodgan said. Lens shoved the shiv in, cut the man's eyeball out neatly.

Bogdan screamed: he didn't scream before. The eyeball, sev-ered from the retinal artery with a flick of the wrist, plopped wetly on the ground, where Lens stepped on it. He pushed Bogdan away from him.

"Do you recognise my authority?" he said.

One by one the men moved away. Bogdan was taken to the infirmary. The same doctor who lost money on Lens kept Bogdan alive, an eye patch now covered the man's empty socket. Later, they sent him to the execution chamber and put a bullet in the back of his head and carted his corpse outside.

Time passed, outside. Inside it was much the same. Lens ate bread, soup. He read Kolpakov, Yefremov, Asimov, Hein-lein, and Clarke, the Strugatskys, and Lem. He cut planks of wood in the lumberyard. He witnessed Kirill as he failed to operate the cutter correctly and his arm disappeared under the blade, bringing forth a fine spray of red mist. He wit-nessed Abram Abramovich beaten to a pulp by the guards, standing over him in a circle, their clubs rising and falling, no sound but their heavy breathing and Abram Abramov-ich's hoarse breath, until it fled. Later in his cell Lens found a tooth embedded in the sole of his shoe. He read Jules Verne.

Every morning they were assembled for roll call under a cold blue sky. They were an island floating alone in a vast space for which there were no charts. He read Wells and

Shelley, Kazantsev and E. E. "Doc" Smith. He murdered Andrei Ionescu, the "Butcher of Brasov," because Mikhail, the stuka, paid him to do it. They sent Lens back to isolation.

When, or how, he got hold of the book, he couldn't later tell you.

17.

"*Lode Stars?*" Dr. Knight said.

"Yes."

Her frowns over time made a flock of seagulls. She said, "Did one of the other prisoners own it?"

"I don't know."

"It was . . . what did you call it? Samizdat?"

"That's right."

"So it could have been smuggled into the prison," she said. "You had visitors, didn't you?"

"Some did. Their visitors were searched."

"Still. You said you did deals with the guards, sometimes."

"Not me. Never me!" Lens said.

"Because you were a vor. A thief."

"A thief-in-law," he corrected her. "I was elected."

Back then there was still a code, he thought. There were laws to live by, not the laws of the Soviet but their own laws, fundamental, constant.

"But others in the prison did receive gifts," Dr. Knight pointed out, unruffled.

"Yes."

"You must have simply acquired the book from one of them and later lost it."

No, he wanted to shout, don't you understand! Years later he sought others like him, and knew this was not just him, not an isolated point on a graph but a part of a pattern, a series of repeatable occurrences. There had even been an article about it, in the *Fortean Times*, sandwiched between an exposé of the royal family as giant lizards and a story about the United States using alien weapons reverse-engineered in Area 51.

In the cell, in isolation, pacing, one, two, three, and turn, one, two, three, and turn, and then it was just there, one day, as though it had always been there: *Putevodnie Zvezdy*, by Yevgeny Hartley: and there was Delia, materialising like the goddess Athena leaping fully formed from her father Zeus' head, in her tiny ship, decelerating into an alien star system. . . .

Lens missed Levi. He sat in the conservatory upstairs and stared out of the windows, loathing the outside, the rising sun, the dawn spreading over the horizon, the stillness of the birds in the trees, the flowers opening to reach the light, their petals spreading. He hated them all, the squirrel staring back at him with sleepy eyes, the scent of wood smoke, the neighing of a horse from the riding school in the distance. Sometimes he wanted to burn it all, just go out there with a soaked rag and a lighter and set it all on fire, the absurdity of it.

It was all just painted backdrop. It was all a sham. Soon the hidden carpenters would come and carry it all away: pick up the horizon and unhook the sun, and what would be left would be a terrible nothingness, and dust, for some reason it made him think of dust.

Which was why he couldn't explain just why he should care about Armstrong, for if nothing was real then Levi, too, was not real, was but a player or, worse, one of *them*, putting on a mask. And yet they were friends.

He wondered uneasily if this had been true before. How much of his existence now was similar to the way he'd lived, he meant the way the real Lens had lived, back on the real Earth when it had still existed, not now, not in the dying light of the universe, this final dusk.

His memory, he wished he could remember more coherently, remember forward as well as back: for instance, his death. He would have liked to remember his death.

"But how do you *know*?" Levi said to him, the time he finally confided, late at night in the pub, with the bartender ringing the bell for last drinks and the last stragglers propping up the bar; they sat by the window, a stack of paperbacks between them. "How do you *know* that what you feel is true?"

Looking at him with concern, and Lens hiding a sense of shame, which he had not felt before, not with anyone.

"I don't," he said. "Not really."

"Have you talked to anyone about it?"

"I've been seeing someone."

"And what did they say?"

"What do you think they said? They think it's a condition. A delusion. Something that began in prison."

"Did you try medication?"

Lens shrugged. "Yes," he said. Yes, he had tried medication. "None worked?"

"Some did." As he spoke he watched the corners. He was always wary of the corners. "Some did," he said, reluctantly. The pills smudged the shadows, muted the whispers in the dark. But they made the whole world grey with them, so that he could see nothing true, could discern nothing real.

"The idea that the universe is a simulation is not exactly new," Levi said. "And there's the holographic principle, the idea that we're encoded in two dimensions, like—"

"A DVD."

"Right. But how do you prove it, I mean one way or the other—"

They were both quite drunk at this point, even though neither man was usually given to alcohol.

"Gents, I'm afraid I'm going to have to ask you to make your way downstairs."

They rose, unsteadily.

"But how do you know time's even real?" Levi said, and they both laughed in the face of the irritated server.

That was the thing, Lens reflected. Levi made him laugh, on some fundamental level he understood Lens, accepted him for what he was. He regretted talking to Levi about the book. He should not have led him down that avenue.

"What if you could prove it," Levi had said. "What if you could prove it, mathematically." He had become obsessed by then, and the obsession had a desperate nature. It was not even real mathematics, it wasn't *abstract*.

———

When the Soviet Union fell they barely knew it, in prison. There were rumours of a coup attempt in Moscow. It was August, and Lens had been again released into the general population and could work in the timber yard, could smell the forest in the distance, could see blue sky. He felt the sun on his naked skin, its warmth, its light.

The Dzerzhinskiy statue was dismantled outside Lubyanka. The red hammer-and-sickle flag was lowered over the Kremlin. It was winter now and the snow fell in thick deadly flurries, and Lens lifted weights, drank tea, sucking the hot liquid through a cube of sugar held between his teeth.

Suddenly there was another world, as though they had shifted sidewise without noticing. Outside the world changed. Inside things remained much the same, only the old dogs on death row had been reprieved: there were no more executions. Five death-row inmates killed themselves on hearing the news. They could not bear the thought of living on, in prison.

Things stayed much the same. On the vory's secret channels, word came of great victories, of new opportunities. The collapse of the Union ushered in an era of legal criminality and endless opportunity: there was money to be made, piles and piles of money. Good men were needed.

Still, nothing changed inside. Lens was calmer, more controlled. He knew now the illusory nature of his prison, which extended far beyond the walls. He had become a Gnostic, for whom the world is the creation not of God but of the demiurge, a mockery, a simulacrum.

He did his time.

The year turned and he was abruptly released. At first he resisted but the guards beat him and dragged him away in shackles to his freedom. As he stepped out of the prison gates a black Mercedes waited for him outside and a man he didn't know at first waited beside it. The man's face split into a wide smile and he opened his arms, saying, "Oskar, Oskar, do you not remember me?"

"Vadim? Can it be you?"

"It is, old friend, it is!"

"But you died, I saw you die, in Afghanistan, on the hard, dry ground, begging for water, your intestines spilling out, held in your hands like sausages."

The man's smile faltered, and his eyes were hard and cruel.

"That never happened, friend," he said softly. "It is true, I was wounded, but I survived, don't you remember?"

". . . Of course," Lens said. "Vadim, it is good to see you, and didn't we always say you had nine lives?"

The man's smile returned to place though his eyes remained dark and unreadable. They hugged. The inside of the car smelled of new leather and Western cigarettes.

They drove a surprisingly short time, to an airstrip at the edge of an abandoned town of timber-built huts. A light plane awaited them there. Lens had never been in a plane before.

From above, Siberia was a mess of spirals and whorls: rivers, clouds and forests mixed together into an impressionist painting. All this time Vadim spoke: he spoke in the car, he spoke on the plane, he spoke in the luxury dacha they arrived in, on the outskirts of Moscow, a newly built palace as gaudy and expensive as a Fabergé egg.

"There is money to be made, Oskar, old friend, for too long you have been inside, the Bratva needs men like you, though it is not the Bratva anymore, not quite, we are now business-men."

"Businessmen?" Lens said, and Vadim shrugged, and slapped him on the back and said, "Come on, let me show you around."

That night under cold bright stars they drank and ate as men patrolled the grounds with machine guns. Vadim explained about the new arms trade, the selling-off of army surplus, the privatisation of oil and gas, but mostly he said, "Do you remember Afghanistan, and the fields of endless poppies?"

"All that red," Lens said. "I had never seen so much red, or so vibrant."

There were girls, too, brought in from Moscow, he had never seen so many beautiful girls and so many empty eyes, and Vadim offered them to him as though they were blini or gingerbread, to be chewed at will.

"Don't tell me you turned bitch in the joint!" Vadim said when Lens refused them, and Lens looked at him, just the once, and said, "I would kill you, Vadim, if you were not already dead."

At that Vadim laughed, and he walked off with three of the girls, and Lens was left alone to watch the dawn: it was his first day of freedom and yet he felt much the same as before.

Then the next day he met the owner of the house, an anonymous bureaucrat with pale blue eyes, thinning hair, and a paunch: the rings on his fingers could buy a neighbourhood in Kitai-Gorod.

"So you are Oskar Lens," he said, "Vadim here has told me so much about you."

"Saved my life, he did," Vadim said, but shifted nervously.

Lens looked at him, saw how scared he was of this man, this nothing, not even a vor. A man without tattoos or rank.

"Is that true?" the man said.

"I suppose," Lens said.

"Afghanistan is of some interest to my organisation," the man said, but he did not elaborate. "I am looking for a good man. I had hoped you were that man."

Lens shrugged. The shadows moved behind this man's eyes, he knew, they had consumed Vadim too, they animated his lifeless body like a puppet. Lens was not fooled, yet he needed work, now that he was free.

Perhaps, we think, what he needed was a purpose.

He had never seen the book again. He'd found it in his cell and lost it, it had vanished with the final line of the book.

They're beautiful, she said.

"What?"

Vadim and he were in the garden. Vadim smoked a joint of Afghan hash. He stared at Lens. "Did you say something?"

Lens fanned the smoke away and didn't answer.

"He likes you," Vadim said.

"He's got no rank, no *name*," Lens said. "He's nothing."

"Don't live in the past, Oskar. This is the future. Why are you smiling? Stop that."

"But I do live in the past."

"Listen, Oskar, he likes you, and we need good men. Men one can trust. These oligarchs, they are the future. The old system's *gone—*"

Frustrated: "I'm talking about an *opportunity*, here."

"It just seems wrong," Lens said. "We took the oath."

"And where did it get you, Oskar? Doing life in Siberia? Come on."

Oskar Lens smiled. Suddenly, everything delighted him. The evening, the stars, the whispering shadows, the guards with their Uzis and the barbed wire walls—

"Well, it's not like you're giving me a choice," he said.

Vadim smiled, too.

"You could walk away," he said.

"And how far would I get?"

Vadim scratched his neck. Lens remembered him dying, a Pashtun bullet in the gut. It was not like he could forget the screams, or the smell of blood, or the dry caked earth. His memory had been like that since that second or third time in isolation, he now thought. It moved all wrong. And he thought they hadn't quite figured it out yet, how linear human memory is, to us it exists all at once. For some reason he thought of a spider's bite.

"You can walk, Oskar. But this is your world. Our world. Don't you want to be rich?"

"Yes," Oskar Lens said. "Yes, I think I'd like that, Vadik."

Vadim smiled at that. "Then come on," he said. "We've business to discuss."

Lens turned over and over that strange, English word. *Business.*

"I suppose you could call it that," he agreed at last.

18.

He was forced to kill Vadim in '98, during the last of the
unfortunate disputes, when Lens' was determinedly making
himself an independent contractor in London. The oligarch
did not last that long, an ex-Spetsnaz team sent by a rival
wiped him out in his car with machine guns on a summer
day just outside of Sochi, alongside his wife, her sister, and
two mousy children.

Fucking Spetsnaz, Lens thought, every second person trying to join up these days was ex-special forces. It was as cheap
to take a hit out on a man as buy a pint of milk in the local
shop.

In Moscow he was retrained: basic English, suits and ties,
expensive watches, a sort of sped-up transformation enacted
by ex-KGB spies just glad to be on someone's payroll.

Accounting, wire transfers, money laundering through real
estate: the international language of money. Lens caught up
quickly. That funny word, business. To celebrate graduation
they drove into Moscow, St. Basil's Cathedral was lit up at
night, in GUM they sold all Western products, just by Red
Square they'd opened a branch of an American burger chain.

They ate greasy burgers and chips and drank strawberry-flavoured milkshakes and Vadim shook his head in wonder and said, "Isn't this the life?"

Then, to bind him further, they travelled past the ring road, where the puddles gathered in the street corners with glowing red and green and yellow dyes, housing estates built on former nuclear waste disposal sites, and there they waited in the dark for a man to pass, and Vadim handed Lens a gun.

"You remember how to use it, don't you?" he said.

Lens did as he was told. When the man lay dead on the ground with his dark blood pooling under his rapidly-cooling body, Lens felt a certain sadness, unexpected and unwelcome. Not at the pointlessness of it all, or that he didn't even know the man's name or what his crime might have been, but for himself, being forced to live this sham of a life in which he was a solitary lantern, one point of light moving amidst endless shadows.

"But you must understand how this sounds," Dr. Knight said. "You must feel deep within you that this is a delusion, else why seek help in the first place?"

"I don't know what to think."

She rubbed the bridge of her nose. Lens told her of days in which creation seemed so bright around him that he had to look away; others when the world dimmed, became grey and insubstantial. He told her of the whispers he heard, sometimes, late at night, as sleep approached. He told her he was tired. He had lived two lives already, after all.

When he first arrived in London the condition lifted for

a little while. The city charmed him, its shabby and genteel antiquity, its low horizon—nothing like Moscow's Stalinist edifices, or the prison's never-ending walls.

Here one could think, one could see, and the clouds covered the sky, day and night, and he seldom had to see the stars.

Product came in, brought over by little old ladies and doctoral candidates and businessmen, inside the hollow frames of baby buggies, posted in statues and books and, once, inside a litter of live puppies.

It came from Afghanistan, smuggled through Turkey and Russia, processed, cut, made its way across Europe, finally, into Lens' hands. He tried it only once, but the drug gave him a dull headache, and in its haze he saw nothing but stars, all the stars in the universe.

He was a reliable manager, he was trusted, as much as anyone could be trusted, he did as he was asked and converted the cash to property, buying up a warehouse here, a shop lease there, a block of flats somewhere else again.

He found Billy first, then Macaroon, young thugs working for old East End hard men, and he took them for his own. He wanted his own men.

He met Barnes early on in his sojourn in London, a sharp and rat-like man with all the useful qualities of a rat, and so he fed him.

Ambition burned him up: to be free, to be himself. He didn't trust the men he had to work with, and he didn't like it when Vadim came over from Moskva, expecting to be picked up at the airport, and entertained with booze and whores, a boy who never grew up, a dead man walking.

Lens started to lay his plans.

He only had one secret. It was harmless, a little hobby, a

way of not being himself, or being himself differently, more fully.

It was an informal meeting of like-minded individuals who gathered every last Thursday of the month at a pub in Holborn, to drink and to talk about books. Not a book club, not exactly. Not a society as such, either. Just an informal drop-in meeting, once a month, everyone invited. They'd begun before the Second World War, and for a while the meetings took place in Arthur C. Clarke's flat on Gray's Inn Road.

Eugene Hartley visited, once or twice, when he was living in London. Kingsley Amis once got into a fist fight with a visiting Fred Pohl over an obscure point of the Three Laws of Robotics, and Michael Moorcock twice got locked in after closing time and drank all the beer.

It was a space for science fiction fans, by science fiction fans. In the past they had called themselves the Circle, or Last Thursday, or the London Group. The name didn't matter, and the location changed from pub to pub, but the meetings remained, uninterrupted, a refuge from the world and its lies, into ones Lens could understand: he could believe in fiction more easily, knowing it was untrue.

The first time he went, he felt such *freedom* that for a moment all the stars in the galaxy couldn't shake, for that one moment, his perfect exhilaration.

He stepped through the pub's threshold almost timidly. Here, he was an unknown, he was a variable in an equation that could take on any value. He was not Lens, the gangster, not Lens, the prisoner. Here he could be no one but himself.

The meeting was upstairs. He climbed the steps and felt a little nervous. Within, people sat in groups, chatted, laughed, drank beer or cider, and he knew none of them. Yet moments later a kind man with white candyfloss hair came up to him, and shoved into his hands a couple of mimeographed leaflets: one was a list of secondhand novels sold by mail order, and the other an advertisement for a convention in Manchester.

They struck a conversation and soon enough Lens was introduced to people, here and there, who looked at him curiously but took him for one of their own.

And for a while he was happy there, talking of outrageous things, space flight and robots, machine intelligence and all that: it was like a drug to him.

We don't understand it. We don't imagine or make believe. All we do is see, for us every reading is a basic truth, an ancient light. We do not understand this pretend.

How can light *lie*?

There was a series of escalating violences as he forged his own path in London, and he cut ties with back home, and for a while there was a siege mentality going on, and they sent men after him, and he had to send them back in parts. Eventually he made a sort of peace, an arrangement, at least, and became his own employer after a fashion.

He did not attend the pub meetings for a while and when he returned, his name had made it into the newspapers a few times, but it made little odds to his fellow fans: what mattered were the books and the wonderful dreams of the future they evoked. In a way, he and the others made for an odd and dys-functional family.

In that family belonged the man Levi Armstrong, with his feverish eyes and his wild dreams of making the impossible real.

"And did not the early writers do exactly that," Levi said. "Didn't Clarke predict the satellite, didn't people land on the moon, don't we have robots, now, and space stations, and computers? It's only a matter of time," he said, warming to his theme, "before we spread out to the rest of the solar system, establish colonies on Mars, mine the asteroids, develop the technology to travel even farther, to the nearby stars, at least, to Alpha Centauri and beyond. Nothing is impossible if you can envision it, if only you can make the math work."

And Lens was captivated by this man, his enthusiasm, his dreams: he alone, it seemed to Lens, was real in this world apart for him, a consciousness preserved from the eaters in some way. They often spoke of Hartley, that strange old sci-fi dreamer: what did he know, how did he dream the things he did?

"Because you see," Levi said, "none of this matters, this expansion into space and living longer, and building machines that could think—none of this matters if none of this is real. If we are not ourselves but copies, echoes of who we once were. In that case," he said, still smiling, delighted with the notion and with himself, "in that case all of this has happened already and we have just forgotten: we're simply living our lives again."

He had not read the book but he knew of it; he was a collector in want of a book. He was as obsessed with the notion as Lens himself was.

But what with the turf war and the attempts on his life, Lens didn't see Levi for a while; when he did the man was changed somehow. More consumed, more desperate. His eyes gleamed brighter. He never asked Lens for drugs, but Lens could tell a user, it was his stock in trade.

He kept this segment of his life a secret, a sliver of him that was for no one but himself. As part of the settlement with the others he quietly stepped out of the drug trade. He had the dirty book shops in Soho and the strip club and two casinos, catering to basic human needs; the dosshouse, a garage, the lending business, the bookies, the warehouse. He was doing all right. He was an immigrant success story. He gave to charity, he moved to the house in Petersham, even though the sky was clearer there and the nights could be difficult. He had a cellar where he often slept. He bought a Persinger device.

Where did Armstrong go? Lens stared out of the glass walls onto the garden. The sun was risen, the garden was a riot of colour. It pained him. It hurt his eyes to watch.

At such moments creation was revealed and it was hard to believe it wasn't real, wasn't all there was. He watched a butterfly flutter across the breeze, deep reds and yellows, with eyes painted on the wings. The eyes watched him.

He stared back at us, seeing our subterfuge. All he wanted was an end to this.

But didn't we tell you, right from the start?

We don't exist.

None of this is real.

———

Alone. He was so alone.

Lens took a deep breath and turned, facing the shadows.

"I'm ready," he said.

The shadows whispered.

Lens came down to the basement, where the helmet waited. The air was filled with ozone, with Daniel Chase's fear, with the traces of Lens' final cigar.

He turned on the machine.

He placed the helmet over his head.

He stared at us defiantly as we gathered in the shadows.

Electricity surged. The magnetic field the device generated was so powerful that it tore Lens' watch off his wrist. The machine began to smoke. Lens sat still.

He was in a small room, without windows. He could smell, impossibly, the smoke from cheap cigarettes, rancid cooking oil. There were many voices, coming and going, and then the voice.

Who was she? What was her name?

The machine hissed with effort. Heat burst from the wiring, melted plastic, caught flame.

Smoke filled the room.

Lens felt her hand on his cheek, for just a moment.

"Mama," he said. "Mama."

The shadows thickened. Lens saw a light burn deep within a bottomless well.

He felt himself change then, become a new thing.

Ahead of him, the dark unknown.

Then, in the distance: the light of a dim red sun, and the circumference of a World around it.

PART FOUR

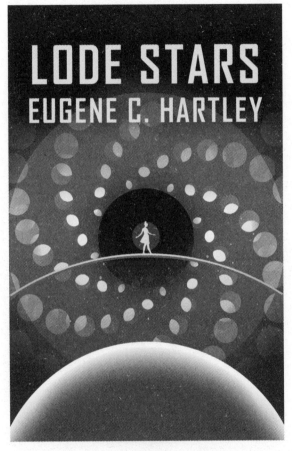

First published by the Fantasy Press, Pennsylvania, 1962.
Reprinted with permission.

19.

One: Ten Thousand Light Years from Home

Delia walked along the circumference of the World and the dim red sun was far below her.

All about her were stars.

The World was constructed in aeons past. The mass of the old planets was combined by long-vanished engineers. The gas giants were dragged from their orbits, their moons trailing behind them like chicks after their mother. Earth and Mars were pushed away and stripped of their elements.

Of the former bodies of the solar system nothing remained but this: the World. A mesh of interlocking rings rotated slowly around the sun at their core. Delia walked along the circumference of the World and thought of her father. News of his passing had caught her unprepared, as painful as gravity.

He died far from there, in the System of the Eyes. The call came at the speed of light. It took ten thousand years to reach her.

Delia walked along the circumference of the World and grieved for her father.

———————

Bees hummed in the garden amongst the flowers. An artificial sun circled this spinning habitat, which floated serenely in the space where Jupiter had once been. The cheerful yellow sun warmed Delia's face.

She washed her face in a stone basin.

When she looked into the water she saw another woman's face looking up at her in confusion, black freckles over translucent skin. The woman's eyes were red. Delia disturbed the water and this image of her other self vanished.

Bees buzzed in the garden. They merged together and coalesced into a humanoid, feminine shape. The shape stood and watched her.

"Well?" she demanded.

"I will go to him," said Delia. She sat up.

"You rather missed the funeral," said Ghis.

"That is not the point."

"It is ten thousand light years away!" protested Ghis.

Delia shrugged, indifferent. "What are time or distance to such as ourselves?" she said.

The bees buzzed and scattered, then reformed. "You can't expect me to accompany you," said Ghis.

"I don't."

The bees roared in anger. "You can't expect me to stay behind!"

"I expect nothing."

Ghis sighed. It was a long-suffering sigh. She stretched her hand, gently. Bees stroked Delia's hair.

"I'll go," said Ghis.

Delia looked up. "You will?"

Ghis snorted. "As if you could be trusted on your own, out amongst the stars!".

The bees parted and scattered between the flowers, and for a time there was silence. The bees, having drunk from the nectar, reformed into Ghis.

"How long has it been since we left the World?" she said.

"Aeons," said Delia. She listened to the gentle murmur of the brook.

"I would like to see mighty Ishtar again," said Ghis, "and hear the star moths sing across galactic space on their strange inexplicable journeys. . . ."

"I would like to speak to my father again," said Delia.

"The Eyes," said Ghis, and the bees shuddered delicately. "I never knew what he saw in that dismal system. It is so far away, with nothing around for light years but dead space."

"Mystery," said Delia, simply.

Ghis sighed. "I suppose. . . ." she said. "How shall we go? Shall we duplicate our consciousness and send it across the Chatter? Though the last time I did that the duplicate came back to see the World again, and we did not get along at all. I would rather not make another enemy of myself."

"We shall go as we are," said Delia. She stood. She was lithe and strong, and Ghis buzzed and the bees surrounded Delia, stroking her on all sides.

"Shall we convert this little worldlet into a vessel?" said Ghis. "It would be pleasant, to travel amongst the stars in luxury."

"I do not care to drag a lunar body across thousands of light years," said Delia. "We shall remake a fraction of its mass and travel in a starship."

"Oh, how *quaint!*" said Ghis.

Delia ignored her. The bees scattered and rose high into the sky, right up against the force-field dome. Tiny white clouds floated serenely in the sky. The brook murmured happily. Delia watched the play of light in water. Through the Chatter, she gave her command. She felt the ground begin to vibrate, gently, as the breaking and remoulding of their tiny worldlet began.

They named their starship the *Tripitaka*, after the ancient monk of that name. Delia watched the World recede behind them.

For a time she meditated in the hydroponic jungle deep in the ship's core. She sat under the great banyan tree and no one disturbed her peace. She thought of her father's journey to the System of the Eyes.

Delia had argued with him. She had asked him not to go. But it did no good. He was searching for something. What, exactly, he wouldn't say.

He departed, frozen, in a tiny comet that streaked across space towards his destination, and his duplicates destroyed their corporeal selves and followed him through the Chatter as pure information. He was not an old-fashioned man but he had some old-fashioned beliefs, and he did not like to spread himself too thin. She didn't even get to keep a part of him.

She had slept for a while; a few thousand years. On waking she became an oarfish and swam the oceans of an alien blue world a few hundred light years away. There was peace in water, and a sort of acceptance.

It occurred to her that there were few mysteries left in the universe. The human race was old: it had survived the nuclear winters, information plagues, and cybernetic revolts of the early millennia, had spread out to the stars, encountered the philosophies and ways of knowledge of a thousand alien species, and learned from them. Humanity was wiser, long-lived, and peaceful. War, humanity had finally learned, was a poor species' choice.

There were few mysteries left, but for the fundamental question of *why*. The universe seemed fine-tuned to bring about the evolution of sentient life.

Where did we come from? wondered a thousand alien species. Why are we here? Is there such a thing as God?

20.

A mere five hundred light years from the former solar system of Earth, there lies a cluster of suns known to humans as the Sevagram. It was there that an offshoot of the School of Without had built, in aeons past, a monastery.

The Without believed God, having created the universe, existed outside of it. The Within, in contrast, believed God was itself a part of the Big Bang, and it was God's particles that made up the universe.

There was little agreement between the space-faring species as to which school was right.

The *Tripitaka* decelerated into the monastery's orbit. Delia, whose thoughts had stretched glacial over the journey (a mere blink of an eye) sped up reluctantly. She had been working on a poem.

The monastery was a huge, ornate structure like a corkscrew spiral, scaly and made of an alien organoform. It twisted and turned in space.

They docked with the structure and entered.

Long corridors whispered with the passage of a dozen alien species. A slug-like creature slithered along the wall, leaving a trail of slime in its wake. The creature was robed in black.

It was a monk.

"We seek the Keeper of Ancient Artefacts," said Delia. She did not know the speech of the Slizni of Sliznyak-4, but her voice bubbled into the Chatter and was converted to Sliznys-kiy, and the monk paused in contemplation then replied.

Delia and Ghis wandered deeper into the edifice. The monastery was ancient. Smooth metal and eternal bricks formed around them into walls that could never be destroyed. The monastery was built long ago by the vanished Daimoni. Dim light came from growing sentient algaeians on the walls. The moss monks murmured to each other and ignored Delia and Ghis.

"Rude," said Ghis.

They got lost several times. A mollusc busy cleaning the floor gave them directions again. They proceeded farther and farther into the bowels of the monastery.

"I do not like this place much," Ghis said, and the bees shuddered delicately. Delia stroked them.

"My father came here," she said.

"Your father kept odd company," said Ghis.

There had been a cryptic note from her father. Delia found it in his personal archives.

For I shall go into the Eye with peaceful intentions, her father wrote. *And assumption of same for the Dwellers in the Dark; but a sentience does not become ascendant without taking precautions; and so I had gone to speak with the Keeper of Ancient Artefacts in the hope of obtaining a working Occlude.*

She could make little sense of it.

Now she walked through the endless dark corridors. They found an elevator that took them down miles and miles at supersonic speed.

A cavernous lair. There were bones on the ground. Delia stepped gingerly.

"It smells," complained Ghis.

Someone coughed in the darkness and turned on a lamp. Delia saw a cave of wonders. Ancient obsolete objects of all kinds piled up everywhere: a rusting positronic robot and a pair of Waldo arms, ansibles and spindizzies, a vat of rare thiotimoline and another of lunarium, two time viewers, a transfer booth and an old General Products spaceship hull, an Axlotl tank and an Ixian probe, Shayolian ears and capsules of Stroon. On and on it went.

Paintings hung on the walls. Delia found herself admiring the image of a girl walking alone on an enormous steel ring that surrounded a dim red sun.

"It is a Bok original," a voice said in the dark. "A survivor from old Earth. Priceless, of course."

Wheels creaked. An enormous creature emerged out of the gloom. The creature was huge, snail-like. A mechanical exoskeleton helped it drag its mass across the floor. The creature left a trail of slime behind it. The wheels creaked as it moved. It raised two feelers and opened large, guileless eyes and looked at them.

"I am Rakso-Snel," it boomed. "I am the Keeper."

Ghis buzzed in reply. The bees scattered, examining the relics.

Delia stared at Rakso-Snel. Saw the black robes the alien wore over its giant frame.

"You are a monk?" she said.

"I am now," said Rakso-Snel. "Yes."

"What were you before?"

The giant monk shook its head.

"I do not rightly know," it said. There was a sense of a dangerous stillness about the creature.

Delia said, "My father came to see you."

"I do not get many visitors," said Rakso-Snel.

"He was seeking an Occlude," said Delia.

The monk was still then.

"The Heresy of the Black . . ." it said at last. Its feelers moved.

"I remember it now, yes," it said. "Yes, someone came. Asking questions. Asking for the device. But I did not have one. I had tried, for a long time I tried, yes. . . . But it was forever out of reach. The man who came to me left disappointed."

Sorrow squeezed Delia's heart in a fist.

"Where did he go?" she whispered.

"There is a place," said Rasko-Snel. "I told him of the story. Perhaps he went there . . . Murkheim, it is called. If you see the man again, wish him well for me."

"He was my father," said Delia. "He is dead."

"Then I am sorry," said Rakso-Snel.

"Do you believe in the God of Within?" said Delia.

"Do I believe everything is a part of God?" said Ghis dubiously. "You, me, a star? Stars are perfectly natural phenomena. They merely obey the natural laws. They form, they burn, they die. The same as us. And besides, I never sensed any *sentience* in a star. I never heard it speak, or write a sonnet, or, well, *do* anything. It just . . . burns."

"You have no heart," said Delia.

"On the contrary, I have many," said Ghis. "They're just small. I also have stomachs and air sacs and venom and stings. But I'm not God."

"You're a cynic," said Delia.

"Bees are naturally cynical," said Ghis complacently.

Behind them, the great monastery spun. Delia's thought processes were already slowing, going Glacial for the journey ahead. Ghis built herself a hive, humming contentedly.

"Do you believe in the Without, then?" said Delia.

"God," said Ghis, "is merely a hypothesis. It cannot be reliably confirmed by experimental data one way or the other."

"Therefore. . . ?" prompted Delia.

"Therefore I don't care," said Ghis.

Delia sighed, then stretched her arms, and Ghis came flying to her. The next several hundred light years passed with the sound of their slow, melodious love-making.

21.

First published separately as "The Occlude" by Eugene C. Hartley in Astounding Science Fiction Magazine, *Dec. 1957*

> Pater Noster, qui es in caelis:
> sanctificetur nomen tuum
> *The Lord's Prayer*

Two: The Occlude

It is said the finest sunsets in the galaxy can be found on the planet Murkheim—as long as you have the money to pay for them. The races of a thousand planets intermingled in Murkheim City, an urban sprawl the size of a continent, and the stolen merchandise of a thousand solar systems could be found in its souks and bazaars.

Delia and Ghis landed at the city's spaceport, a vast hour-glass-shaped building rising out of the clouds of the planet Murkheim. The bees that were Ghis expanded and contracted in a protective cloud around Delia as they descended from the top of the spaceport into the world below. They were in free fall, dropping down a vast chute, alongside fellow passengers and crates of cargo. Delia nodded politely to a group of Gzant, who blinked at the two of them curiously. The Gzant resembled lychees with eyes, and hung from their travel pods on long strings of naturally secreted, sticky mucus-like material. They were clad in opulent diamond-fabric cloth that marked them as wealthy merchants.

"How goes the Gzant exodus?" said Delia, after pleasantries were exchanged.

"Last we heard," said a wizened old Gzant, "the swarm had taken a decision to venture across intergalactic space to the next galaxy. It is a journey of some two and a half million light-years, so it should take a while. But even a journey of such length must begin with a single light-minute, as the saying goes."

"Indeed," murmured Ghis, on a private channel to Delia, and Delia hid a smile.

"May I ask," said Delia, "if you have ever heard of a device called an Occlude?"

The old Gzant turned his large, innocent eyes on Delia.

"Never," he said, solemnly. "But if it is exotic technology you are after, try asking at the Quarter of Artificers, in the south of the city. Much that is forbidden elsewhere can be had, here on Murkheim, for a price."

"This is a fool's errand if ever I saw one," said Ghis. But she said it privately, in Delia's ear only. Delia sighed and, in silence, they dropped through the warm, humid air, watching as they passed below the clouds and the city emerged into view.

A thousand races had built and rebuilt Murkheim over the

long millennia. Even as Ghis and Delia watched, giant spider-like machines moved over the horizon, patiently arranging and rearranging buildings, factories, and power plants. Tall minarets of some alien metal rose into the sky and the air was filled with flying vehicles. The city spread to the horizon, until land ended and the ocean began.

Delia breathed in Murkheim's air. It felt good to be back in one of the galaxy's busy hubs, away from the dying sun of Sol, away from that small and insignificant solar system on the edge of the galaxy that was notable only, and if at all, as the birthplace of an obscure species called humanity.

They were some three thousand light-years from home. Delia thought uneasily of her father's cryptic note.

"Just what are these Dwellers he mentions, who sit all alone in the dark?" said Ghis.

"He seems to have been writing in code," said Delia uncertainly.

Their detour to Murkheim had taken some time, but time has little meaning to the near-immortal. Their long drop to the surface slowed as the antigrav devices took gentle hold, and they landed on the planet with an easy step. The vast doors of the spaceport were forever open, and Delia and Ghis passed through them and into the city itself.

The continent that housed Murkheim City was bisected by the planet's equator. The air was scented with vanilla and seaweed, ozone bursts and frying, exotic meats, with rot and rust, with oil and tar. As they walked down the wide avenues of the city Delia watched the fronts of shops, straining for a hint of humanity. She saw the window of the Solar Spice and Liquors Company, an Isher weapons shop, and an outlet for the respected Encyclopedia Galactica Foundation.

When at last they reached the Quarter of Artificers, planetary night had fallen, and the sky was lit by the three moons of Murkheim, which suddenly seemed to Delia like bright eyes, watching her. Frightened, she pulled Ghis into the shadow of a high stone wall.

"What is it?" said Ghis.

"Nothing," said Delia. When she next dared look, they were only moons in the sky, nothing more. Yet a sense of unease permeated her thoughts.

It was quieter in the Quarter of Artificers. It was an old part of the city, the ground paved with uneven slabs of grey-white stone. The quarter was dominated by a gigantic temple complex, dedicated to the God-from-Without.

Eldritch lights burst into flames high above, sending down showers of bright sparks. The air grew thick with a powerful chemical miasma. Tiny mechanical beings ran and wheeled and flew through the streets, chattering and yabbering in a nonsensical singsong of machine talk, and in a corner under the walls of the great temple, a group of cowled aliens watched Delia and Ghis from the shadows.

"I do not like the look of them," said Ghis.

"But they're not doing anything," protested Delia.

"Exactly," said Ghis.

The shops in this part of the city were ill-lit and low-ceilinged. They tried asking at several artificiers, yet each sent them, with shakes of the head and vague promises of success, deeper and deeper into the quarter. The lanes grew ever more narrow, and turned and twisted, often leading them to dead ends and blind alleys. Both noticed that the cowled creatures were following them, and though neither commented further on that fact, Delia found herself increasingly reaching for her weapon.

Finally, at a little stall displaying Heechee artefacts of dubious provenance, a wizened old Tweel told them, in her curious language of clicks and barks, that she thought the answer they were seeking might be found within the temple complex itself.

"Occlude," she said. "It is a curious term . . . one I had not heard for centuries."

"Do you know what it is?" said Ghis eagerly. Delia was uncomfortably aware of their shadows. She thought of her father, then. They had spent two centuries living in Ishtar, the mighty empire at the heart of the galaxy, and one decade he had taken her to Viola Siderea, the robber planet; she remembered, suddenly and acutely, walking with him that long afternoon in the thieves' bazaar, how he held her hand, insisting on taking human form. They had strolled together, admiring the stolen wealth of long-lost planets, and she had felt happy and safe just being with him and having him in her life. She had not thought of that particular moment for centuries, and she felt an ache in her heart that she had tried to suppress, ever since the news came of her father's death.

Where are you, Father? she thought. *What have you* done?

"I heard the term used, only once," the old Tweel said. She looked at them doubtfully. "A passing reference, a long time ago and far from here, on an orbital station which was soon after destroyed. It was a time of civil war in that part of the galaxy, on the edges of space. I was a soldier, then. What the war was about I no longer remember. No doubt it was important to us at the time.

"One day, a starship appeared as though out of nowhere and docked at the station. It was a black ship, as black as night, and its passengers were human. I had not seen humans before, and I was young, and curious. I was seconded to their security detail. They must have had some clout, I remember thinking, for what business of ours was it, to offer hospitality to strangers at a time of war? Below us the planet was being destroyed, and the war had spread even to the outer system and across the moons.

"There were three of them. They wore black, with hoods over their heads. They were partly augmented with machinery, but that was not unusual.

"Food was brought to them. I tried to eavesdrop on their conversation, but my translator was ill-equipped for human speech and I could barely understand them. I understood only snatches: that they were priestesses, of some secret order of the God-from-Without; they had come from a place far away, a strange and anomalous region of space occupied by nothing but what we call the Destroyers, and which they called lode stars."

"The Eyes. . . ." whispered Delia.

The Tweel looked at her sharply.

"Yes," she said.

"Did they mention an Occlude?" demanded Ghis.

"They mentioned a device. At first I thought it was a weapon but it was not a weapon as such. It was a protective device, though what shape it took, or what its purpose was I could not tell you. But they carried it, I was convinced of that, and they were being pursued. Where they came from, such a thing was heretical. This much I learned and no more. The next planetary rotation they were gone, and a month later the station was destroyed and we were scattered across nearby space. I abandoned soldiering soon after that."

The Tweel sighed. "I was younger then," she said. "I do not know where they went or what happened to their cargo. But this is Murkheim, through which all the treasures of the galaxy, sooner or later, must pass. Take your quest to the temple, but be careful: for they are peculiar there, and they discourage strangers. Ask for the Blind Sister, yet be careful of her gaze. She had lost her sight to a supernova on the mad Von Ray expedition, and now sees farther than us, and into stranger realms than these. This is all I know."

The two companions thanked her. The bees came and landed softly on Delia's shoulder and braided themselves into her hair, whispering that this was all folly, yet Delia and Ghis proceeded along the high walls of the temple complex, until they reached the locked and narrow gates that led within.

22.

"Ghis!" shouted Delia. Over the ruined courtyard of the alien temple the vultures circled like planes. In the centre of the courtyard stood a giant statue of the God-From-Without, a formless expressionist creation modelled in metal and stone, its constituent parts fading and emerging into being as they passed through hidden dimensions.

"Delia, help me!" cried Ghis. The roar of the bees was angry, panicked. The kidnappers contained Ghis's multiple struggling bodies within a powerful force field. They fled across the gigantic grounds of the temple compound as Delia gave chase. The kidnappers were small, rat-like creatures, with great yellow eyes and carefully coiffed whiskers. In desperation, Delia pulled out her gun. She began to fire bolts of pure energy at the retreating kidnappers, who rode tiny, electric train engines along a maze of ancient tracks that lay in a confusing profusion all over the compound ground.

"Stop!"

A bolt of energy hit one of the aliens. The creature and toppled from its ride. The rest of the pack sped away towards the shadows of the great walls and were soon lost from sight.

Only Ghis's final cry still echoed in the fetid air.

Pain and fear gripped Delia. She would not let herself think of Ghis's fate. Not now. She ran to the fallen alien and knelt by its side. The creature looked up at her, its yellow eyes turning red with blood. Its whiskers twitched. There was a hole in its chest, and through the hole Delia could see the bio-mechanical insides. The creature was half-machine!

Oil and blood leaked out of the creature, soaking into the ground. The air reeked of electricity and metal.

"Where is she?" demanded Delia. She shook the creature roughly, shoving her gun in its face. "What have you done with Ghis?"

The alien stared into her eyes.

"You will . . . never . . . obtain the . . . Occlude!" it hissed.

"Where is she! Tell me or I'll shoot!"

The creature's yellow-red pupils nictitated . "You must . . . desist . . . from your quest." Then it hissed, a long, shuddering exhalation of air, and its eyes closed. It was dead.

Delia sat back heavily. She hugged her knees, the useless gun still in her hand, the dead creature by her side.

How had it come to this? she wondered, numbly. And what would she do now?

23.

"Tell me," demanded Delia. "Tell me where she is!"

The Blind Sister huddled in the corner of the stone-walled room, in the deep dark recess where the shadows whispered. She looked like a pile of twigs, bound together by the black robes of those who worshipped the God-from-Without. She had two blind eyes and a third: a glittering gem embedded in her forehead, in which bands of purples and reds swirled and spiralled. It was this eye that examined Delia, seeming to pierce into her very soul.

"How far would you go?" the Blind Sister said, and her voice brought to mind the vast graveyards of abandoned fleets, of the dead hulls of giant ships floating broken and empty between the stars.

"How far would you go, Delia of Sol, to bring back the ones you love?"

Delia sank to the soft, dank ground.

"Tell me," she whispered. "And I would cross God and Death itself to bring them back to life."

The Blind Sister extended her hand. In her palm she held a black crystal orb. As Delia watched she began to discern in its darkness the tiny lights of suns and galaxies, forming and growing, burning, giving life.

Then they began to fade out and die; and at last Delia saw the lights form spirals around a great, central darkness, an impossible hole that could bend light and time itself to it, and she shrank from it in horror, gasping, "No, no!"

She felt it *notice* her, and the world turned dark, a profound darkness in which no light, no life, no love had ever, could ever have, existed, and she was no longer in the room but lost in a dark maze; and she knew the name of the maze was death.

"I'm coming, Ghis, I'm coming for you!" she said. She took a step into the darkness, and then another and another, until the maze swallowed her whole.

Malformed torches spluttered high in their alcoves on the stone walls; the flames cast grotesque shadows over the inner temple hall. It was a vast, cold space, grimy with the dust and residue of centuries; the stones, it was said, were brought from the dying hell of Paradise IV itself. In the far end bees hummed, trapped inside tiny metal containers. The sound of a thousand furious bees filled the air and Delia's heart leapt in her breast and she cried, "Ghis!"

"Come forth, Delia of Sol," said the voice. As Delia moved forward, small, rat-like figures materialised. The strange creatures she had fought before carried short, stubby weapons, aimed at her with a cold professionalism.

Delia walked, head held high. Deeper and deeper she went into the inner temple, until she stood before the dark. There was a figure in the shadows, up on a raised dais, but what manner of alien creature it was she could not tell.

"You have kidnapped my companion," she said. "I come for her release."

Laughter, cold and mocking, rolled out of the shadows until it filled the hall.

"But this is not all you came for, Delia of Sol," accused the voice.

"No. It is not," said Delia.

"You come as a thief in the night!" The voice was old, tinged with tar and smoke. "What right do you have, Delia of Sol, to stomp your way here, into the inner sanctum of the God-from-Without, seeking Occlusion?"

"I come by right of grief," said Delia quietly. "I come claiming the protection of Occlude, in the name of my father who went into the Eye."

The acolytes hissed as one, and drew from her as though she were poisoned.

"The Eye!"

"You know of whom I speak?"

There was a long silence. Then, "Yes. . . ." said the voice, and it sounded weary now, and terribly old. "An Earthman. He came here, long ago. I see his likeness in your eyes. We—I almost forgot him."

The shadows shuddered. The rat creatures stepped back in unison. Their bright eyes shone in the torchlight. The shadows moved, and out stepped the unseen speaker.

Delia stared.

It was an ancient, withered Earth woman.

"I warned him not to go," said the woman. Her eyes were blue, the startling blue of vanished oceans. "But he was a stubborn man, your—father?"

"Yes."

"We are sorry about your friend," the old woman said. She flicked her wrist and the metal boxes sprang open.

The bees that were Ghis exploded out of their captivity and coalesced into an angry cloud. Delia extended her arms and Ghis flew to her, the bees landing on her shoulders and arms.

"I'm so sorry, Ghis."

"We protect it, you see," the woman said. "Strangers who come asking unwanted questions are not welcome."

"You knew him," Delia said. "You knew my father."

"Yes." A small, tired smile briefly illuminated the woman's face. "He, too, walked the maze of death to reach here. He could be very persuasive, your father."

"But what was he afraid of? What exactly *is* the Occlude?"

"I do not rightly know," the woman said, "the answer to your second question. Occlusion is a thought, perhaps. A formulation. Or perhaps it is a device. Things get confused, where time and space press so close together. As for the first . . . we believe lode stars are eyes, yes. God's Eyes. They absorb all matter and all light, compressing it into a singularity. For aeons we believed this was all there was, and civilizations rose and fell and went into the Eyes willingly, ready to be seen by the God-of-Without.

"Yet life can take root anywhere. And we discern that lode stars, for all the matter that they take, also emit a strange form of radiation. For too long we thought nothing of it. Yet now, some believe it is *communication*. Someone, or some thing, is trying to speak to us from within the Eyes. Only it is not speech, exactly. The matriarchy in the System of the Eyes had studied the lode stars for generations. And as they tried to comprehend the patterns embedded deep within this *leakage*, they came to an awful conclusion.

"The material, it was psychic wastage. Random memories; jumbled, fleeing thoughts; the broken fragments of many lives."

The old woman stared at Delia with her guileless, terribly blue eyes.

"It was not communication at all," she said at last, and sighed; a sound as empty and awful as space. "It was *leftovers*."

A storm of meteorites as bright as embers flared overhead and was gone.

"I cannot *show* you the Occlude," the priestess said. She advanced on Delia and abruptly took Delia's face in her hands. Her eyes stared deep into Delia's own.

"But I can *give* it to you!" she said. She leaned in to Delia's body, her hands dry and warm on Delia's face. Her lips closed on Delia's, and a terrible coldness came pouring out of her mouth, questing at first into Delia's mouth like a tongue, then becoming a great bellow, a cold and empty nothingness that poured from the old woman's mouth into Delia's body, filling it, filling her with its unnameable aura until Delia could see, know, nothing, and she gasped, for she knew only the coldness of dying.

". . . *Enough!*" cried Ghis. Only belatedly did Delia hear her.

When she returned to herself, she was lying on the temple ground. The rat-like monks were gone. The old priestess lay beside her, spent and dying. The bees that were Ghis flew every which way in an angry confusion.

"I had waited so long. . . ." the old priestess said. "Now, you shall bear the burden of the Occlude!"

Her eyes rolled back her smile was smoothed clean away until her mouth was at rest. She breathed out one last, cold shudder, and Delia shied from it in horror and despair.

She could feel it, could feel it inside her now—the Occlude!

24.

Three: The Eyes of the World

It is said there is nothing in the universe more beautiful than a lode star as it gathers matter onto itself. Three light years from Third Eye, Delia and Ghis watched the ebbing flow of cosmic dust as it swirled around the black hole.

You who remember Earth, think of it as all of its matter—its oceans, continents, its humans and trees—compressed into a mote of dust. Now picture that speck as it joins all the others of millions of worlds that were born, have lived, and died in the universe. *That* was the swirling nebula here at the end of the universe.

This matter—this *information*—circled the lode star, which resembled a dark eye; and Delia suppressed a shudder, for it felt to her as though the Eye was watching her; and with the quiet knowledge, moreover, that it would soon know her, absorb her unto itself, as it had consumed so many others over untold aeons.

Behind the Eye, the field of stars shone in the darkness of space like billions of tiny fireflies. Everywhere you looked, there was still life, there was still light. As stars died others were born, yet all, the Eye seemed to suggest, were mortal, all would live, flare up, and die, and all return to whence they came from, to the primordial dark from which no light can escape.

"I hate it," said Delia, viciously, staring at the Eye. "I hate it!" The bees hummed comfort all about her.

"Yet it is also beautiful," said Ghis softly.

The air was stale in the Observatory around Third Eye: it smelled of seared steak and hot metal, as though the space station's air filters had stood too long without being replaced, so that they had begun to let in the smell of space. Delia made a small adjustment in her physiognomy and the smell faded away, but she was still somehow *aware* of it, and Ghis flew here and there in a chaotic hive of agitation.

They had travelled ten thousand light-years from home to this desolate corner of space. The three lode stars dominated everything. The Matriarchy alone inhabited the system: their habitats and starships were tiny pinpricks of light in the vacuum.

"It's a dump," said Ghis.

"It is old," a voice said.

Delia turned; Ghis took flight. Behind them, a golden avatar materialised.

It was shaped like a woman, with gold, metallic skin and black, fathomless eyes, with no pupils or irises, nothing but perfectly featureless discs.

The bees hissed angrily, startled.

"It is old, and worthy of your respect," the avatar said. "Your father spent much of his time with us here, Delia, in this very orbital. He loved it here."

The avatar turned its head this way and that, observing them with its disconcerting eyes.

"I am Grand Aunt Dorothea," it said.

"You are Aunt Dorothea? Where is your Primary?" said Delia.

"She is on Homelight, three light-years away. She has been in seclusion for over a century, contemplating the Deeper Mysteries of our order. I am her go-to for the corporeal world. As far as you are concerned, I *am* her."

"You knew my father?" said Delia.

"You must understand, for us this has happened millennia ago," said Dorothea. "Time passes slowly, the closer one is to the Eye. Sometimes we pass centuries this way, in the blink of an Eye, within the time dilation zone. Your father used to ride a Cyclops."

"A Cyclops?" said Delia.

"A one-person observation pod," said Dorothea. "They were built long ago, for manoeuvring close to the Eyes. Your father spent an eternity near the lode stars. He had visited all three, but this is the biggest. It is the one he went into. One day, many aeons from now, the Eyes will merge; and sooner or later all matter in the universe will converge into a single, all-seeing Eye. . . ."

For all of the avatar's metallic voice, Delia thought, it had the crazed tone of a fanatic; and it made her shiver, and the bees that were Ghis, sensing her discomfort, settled around her in a protective cloud, their stingers aimed at the avatar.

"What did he study?" asked Delia, quietly. "How did he die?"

"He was alone in the Cyclops around the eye, meditating. In his last few centuries, Delia, your father developed some fanciful notions. Who can tell? The sharpest mind grows dull with the turning of the tides and the ageing of the stars. He began to spend much of his time skirting close to the gravitational pull. He must have simply come too close, realised too late that he couldn't turn back."

The avatar shrugged. "I am sorry you have travelled all this way in vain. He is gone, Delia of Sol; he is gone into the Eye of God. I know he went gladly when he realised, knowing he will at last be Seen. What more is there to say, or want?"

Delia said nothing. The avatar nodded, then turned and left. Delia stared out at the distant Eye.

It looked back mockingly.

"She lies!" hissed Ghis. "She knows the truth of his passing."

Delia said nothing. Pain gripped her heart.

She stared at the Eye.

"Oh, Father," she murmured. "Oh, Father, lama sabachtani!"

25.

From space, Homelight was a welcoming beacon in the dark.

Come closer, however, and the worldlet's more unsettling features became visible. Green metal pyramids rose out of the pockmarked surface, glowing faintly with an eldritch light, and there were deep gashes carved into the surface of that artificial world, like the runes of an ancient, lost alphabet.

"How ghastly," said Ghis.

"It's not so bad," said Delia.

Somewhere down there, Delia knew, her father had toiled in study for centuries. Somewhere down there, where the Grand Lodge held power, her father had found what he sought. From there he departed, for the last time, to Observatory, and from there into the Eye. . . .

Yet they could find no answers. Nothing but a cool politeness, insincere condolences, an endless procession of black-clad Aunts and their disciples and progeny, the short-lived Sacrifice.

In their time on the Observatory, Delia and Ghis watched many of the tiny beacons launched towards Third Eye: willing Sacrifice going into God's Eyes to be Seen.

"It is barbarous and inhumane," said Ghis vehemently.

Now they stared down on Homelight as their small craft approached. The green pyramids shone wetly in the faint starlight.

The planetoid's gravity caught them and they slid into its orbit until a rune like a squid's black eye opened wide and they descended into the body of the world itself.

"What did you find in the Archives?" said Delia. It was months later. "Is my father mentioned?"

"Your father," said Ghis, and her humming grew louder and angry. "Your father, Delia, does not exist. There is nothing in the databanks about him. His very presence here was erased."

Delia stood still, gazing at the alien stars outside.

"It was just like him," she said angrily. "To vanish like this, to take risks, to . . . step into this nest of fanatics and not make plans beyond. To leave me. He was always good at leaving."

The bees that were Ghis parted and remerged. She buzzed reassurance.

"There was one thing," she said.

Hope flared in Delia's heart.

"A tale for children," said Ghis. "From centuries past. Long after your father was here. Long before we arrived."

A sharp pain afflicted Delia, like a ghost within her, trying to wake up.

"What did it say?"

"It recounts the tale of a man who travelled into the Eye," said Ghis. *"For in his delusion he became convinced of living beings on the cornea of God's Eye; and so he set into the Eye to speak with them, and became a Sacrifice.* The illustration is of a knight, or a fool, and he carries in his hand a bright lamp as he descends into the event horizon."

"What does it mean?" said Delia; but a chill stole over her heart.

"They knew," Ghis said, with certainty. "They knew of the eaters all along."

"And they had used him? My father?"

"That," a new voice said behind them, startling them both. "You would have to ask me, my dear."

They turned, and saw Grand Aunt Dorothea. Not the un-changed avatar from the Observatory, but the person itself: this ancient creature of flesh and blood.

Pale rotting skin flapped loosely over her tall and bony skeleton, and her mouth was stretched in a rictus of a smile, revealing yellowed, broken teeth. Delia drew back with a hiss of distress, and the bees that were Ghis coalesced about her protectively.

"You!" said Delia.

"Well?" said the apparition. "Wat did you wish to ask me, Delia of Sol?"

"Tell me," said Delia. She stared at the grotesque creature and felt all the anger and sadness that she'd pushed deep inside her rise to the fore.

"Tell me, how did my father die?"

26.

Grief, ten thousand light years from home, pressed on her without warning.

Aunt Dorothea stood at the window.

"He knew the risks," she said.

"You knew his plan," said Delia. "It was not an accident."

"No," agreed Grand Aunt Dorothea. "It was not an accident. He chose to go."

"A Sacrifice."

"No. Never that. An explorer, perhaps. An emissary, rather."

Delia closed her eyes. "How long have you known?" she whispered.

"Known? We have never *known*," said Aunt Dorothea, sharply. "We have only ever suspected."

"The entities?"

"Lode stars such as these suck all matter, all light," said Dorothea. "Yet, somehow, they also emit a radiation of their own. For aeons we believed this to be nothing more than noise, a hum, but recently . . . in the past Galactic Year or so we began to suspect differently. Your father was drawn by the rumours. Other races must have deciphered the whispers emanating from the lode stars in past cycles. Civilizations now extinct, gone into the Eyes of God. We all travel towards extinction. What lies beyond the blue event horizon? Nobody knows."

"You were *listening* to them?" said Ghis. "The entities?"

"There is a constant stream of data, of radiation. It makes no sense on the whole. But sometimes, just sometimes, we'd catch glimpses of meaning. The entities refer to this radiation as 'waste.' We do not know how they evolved. There was nothing to suggest harm, at first . . . but we are a suspicious race, us humans. And there are warnings, if you know where to look. Cryptic references. A black monolith on an ice-moon round Procyon. A beacon still broadcasting in a dead alien tongue, embedded in the core of Tau Ceti. A wall carving within a cave on a nameless planet in the Vega system.

"For aeons we attempted to decipher the meaning in the data. We became uneasy. Long before your father came we . . . there was a schism. Don't forget that all this while, our people went into the Eyes. All we do, all we are, is ultimately plunged into the whirlpool of night. And so we sat, and waited, for a signal, some sort of sign. Yet none came.

"Only, sometimes, an echo. A weird, unsettling cry, a warbling voice: one of us, driven mad with despair. We were uneasy, yes. We began to suspect that we were being. . . ."

"Eaten," whispered Delia.

"Yes."

"You went looking for protection."

"We thought it worthwhile to take precaution. There were those of us who objected. Who saw any attempt to Occlude before God as a sin. We did not . . . war . . . as such. But there was conflict."

Delia thought of the old Tweel they met on the planet Murkheim. Of the alien's curious tale, of the three women who had
come from far away, carrying a secret with them. . . .

"It was you," she whispered. "On Murkheim."

"Not me, child," said Grand Aunt Dorothea, severely. "Ren-
egades. They had stolen the thing. I cannot tell you what it is,
exactly. A device, or an alien way of thinking. Perhaps it is a
metaphor, but for what, I do not know. The product of all our
research, our final line of defence, if such were needed. It was
stolen, and for millennia lost. Until your father came to us."

The hush in the room was profound but for the rapid beat
of Ghis' wings. The room smelled of old books, the smell of
wet cat fur and vanilla.

"You sent him to his death," Delia whispered. "You sent
him into the lode star to die."

"To *live!*" said Dorothea. "To survive! To *be*, Delia! To exist
forever as a recursive pattern of pure information, aswirl in
the light of a myriad of dying stars. . . ."

Delia blinked back tears; her vision swam. Beyond the window meteorites fell in a never-ending shower of sparks.

"Does my father *live?*" she said.

Grand Aunt Dorothea sighed.

"That's . . . a matter of interpretation," she said.

"I guess this is goodbye," said Ghis awkwardly.

Delia nodded numbly.

"You are sure?" said Ghis.

"Yes."

"I cannot come with you."

"I don't expect you to," said Delia.

"Then it is goodbye."

Delia turned her face. The bees hummed all about her, a parting kiss. Then they fled the room and Ghis was gone.

Delia was alone.

She entered the Cyclops. It rose into the air and Delia silently initiated the airlock sequence.

The Cyclops shot out of the porthole, away from the Observatory and into space.

Delia watched the orbital recede away. Ghis was there, but Ghis would recover, they had each lived long years, there had been other partings, other pained goodbyes.

The Cyclops bobbed like an apple in a stream as it was pulled to the Eye. She would survive, in some form, Delia thought. She was protected. Like her father she was in possession of a working Occlude.

Soon the starlight was swallowed whole. The Eye waited, the mass of dismantled worlds revolving in patient swirls.

Soon the gravitational tide would rip her apart atom by atom. Soon everything that was Delia would cease to exist.

Soon. . . .

Delia fell into the lode star.

PART FIVE

EUGENE CHARLES HARTLEY: A LIFE

27.

1921

Once there was a man who fell into the eye of God, and he became a little boy.

This is how it starts, or how it ends, I can no longer recall. This is just a story I used to tell myself when I was little. Lying in the attic of my grandparents' house in Montana, I would curl up in the small camp bed that was mine alone, and read with a flashlight under the covers. I told myself that I was someone else, someone powerful. I wasn't really Eugene Charles Hartley, whose father was away to sea and rarely home, whose mother was of a nervous disposition, as they said back then. I wasn't at all little Gene, who was afraid of shadows and the monsters who lived in the attic and only came out at night.

I was an old soul, immortal, a traveller from the far future come to Earth to save humanity, a noble messiah. No one knew who I really was, but I knew. I knew that I was special.

1925

The older kids picked on me again. They laughed at me and kicked me. I cried, not from the pain but from the unfairness of it all. I was smarter than them! I was *better*! The house was cold when I got back. Father was away again. Mother was in her room. I sat alone and read adventure stories. I could lose myself in the stories and become someone else. When I got hungry I went into the kitchen to get cereal and milk. An alien thing, like a sack of dark ink, was chewing on the furniture. Whatever it touched disappeared and became a lost in the nothingness of which it itself was part. I froze. It noticed me, turned what passed for a head and saw me. I thought it would eat me, too, but it vanished instead. It was as though it and I could somehow understand one another. I fetched a bowl of cereal and sat at the counter, the tears dry on my face.

1929

College was fun but I didn't do well. I almost never dreamed about the shadows—the eaters as I'd come to call them. I took all kinds of courses, in atomic physics and in the science of the mind. I raised money from my fellow students to purchase a boat, but the money went missing and so did the boat. I couldn't explain it—it was just one of those things. But with one thing and another I didn't go back to school when the new term started.

1934

I picked up every pulp magazine I could find and read through them. They were junk, and I knew I could do better. As Susie got bigger and bigger I got to bashing out words on my trusty Underwood. It wasn't long before I got a check for $150 from *Thrilling Adventures* and then another for $100 from *The Phantom Detective*. It was more money than I'd ever seen before.

We named the baby Eugene Jr. when he came. He was a sickly boy, but he was mine and I loved him.

But I had to make a living. At that time I still only thought of myself as a writer, though I already knew I was a great one. I took the train to New York, rented a cheap room at the Forty-Fourth Street Hotel, and set about becoming the King of the Pulps. I used to have a table at Rosoff's, then catch some drinks at the White Horse Tavern where all the old boys hung out. I impressed the hell out of them, even Lester Dent, the guy who wrote *Doc Savage*. I could out-type, out-drink, out-smoke, and outsell any of those guys, and didn't they just know it!

1940

Before the war broke out I was living in California. Susie and the kids were in Montana, living near my grandparents, but I didn't want to go back. I was writing, and getting paid, and it wasn't really my fault Susie had got pregnant in the first place, was it?

LAVIE TIDHAR

Jack Parsons owned this massive house in Pasadena and I took to staying with him most of the time. Jack was a rocket scientist and an occultist. He was working at Cal Tech, and building rockets in the backyard. The Heinleins, Robert and Leslyn, used to come around often, as did some of the other SF writers who lived nearby—Cleve Cartmill, Jack Williamson, "World Wrecker" Hamilton. There were always girls hanging around, and many of Jack's friends from the Agape Lodge, the local chapter of the occult order headed by Aleister Crowley, as well as his rocket enthusiast friends from Cal Tech.

We used to have parties in the backyard late into the night, drinking highballs and beer, smoking—there'd usually be someone passing a marijuana cigarette around, and more often than not I, too, would partake. It was Jack, I think, who first told me about the hole in Einstein's equations—how there were these theoretical "dark stars" whose mass compressed into a gravitational field so strong that it would not only bend light but absorb it, and in which the laws of physics themselves eventually broke down within the eye of the star, its singularity.

The idea excited me in ways I was unable then to articulate. It was as though rather than learning it for the first time I was rediscovering it, like hearing a half-remembered song. The idea of the dark stars arose strange feelings in me, of fear but also of longing. Later at that party, drunk and a little stoned, I was chatting to a beautiful brunette when a man who was roughly my age, dressed peculiarly in blue jeans like someone in a B-movie western, bumped into me.

"Watch it, you fool!" I said, but he just stood there and gaped at me, as though I were some alien landed on Earth (which gave me an idea for a story).

"I can see your face," he said in wonder.

"Yeah? So? I can see yours," I said, and the brunette beside me (I'd already forgotten her name), laughed when I said, "and it ain't all that pretty, either."

"You're Hartley," he said, unfazed. "The writer."

I must admit I preened a little at that. "You have read my work?"

"I read all of your books," he said.

"But I have not written any," I said, my smile remaining fixed around my cigarette. The brunette laughed again, then excused herself and went to the makeshift bar, where she got chatting to Anthony Boucher, that swine (years later I heard he wrote a novel about us all, from that time. It was one of those dreadful murder mysteries, and I appeared as some improbably named creature who does nothing but seduce young women while boasting of the speed of his writing—well, I never troubled to look up a copy, myself).

"But you will," the man said. He kept looking at me, as though he'd never seen a man before. "You'll write many books, and you will become very successful, and famous, and rich."

"You sound like a fortune teller," I said, laughing, though he was making me feel ill at ease. "Would I go on a long journey, too?"

"I . . . I think so," he said.

"Where are you from?" I said. "Are you one of the Cal Tech boys?"

"No," he said. He really did look very confused, and I wondered just how much he'd had to drink already, though I can't say as I had noticed him before. "I think I'm from the future."

"Nice, is it?" I said.

"What?"

"Nice there? The future?"

"Oh." He shrugged. "It's all right, I guess," he said.

I pointed at his clothes. "Is this how they dress? In the future?" I said.

He glanced down. "I guess, sure," he said. "Listen, I don't know how much time I have. I must get hold of your book, you see. I've been looking for it for a long time."

"But I told you already," I said, and this time I dropped both the smile and the cigarette. "I haven't written any yet."

"But I really must have it," he said, and he looked so stricken that I almost felt sorry for him. Whatever play he was running it clearly wasn't working for him.

"If you're really from the future," I said, "tell me who's going to win the World Series this year."

"What year is it?" he said, then, before I could even answer (I'm not sure what I would have said), he added, "Anyway, it doesn't matter. I don't really follow baseball."

"You're English?" I should have recognised his accent. He nodded. "Then tell me something else. Will we enter the war with Germany?"

"Oh, yes," he said. "Soon, I think."

"Will we win? Or are there only Nazis in the future?"

"Oh, it all works out, I think," he said, vaguely.

"Is there anything you can tell me about the future?" I said, growing irritated. He clearly wasn't much of a conversationalist.

"I don't know," he said. "I mean, it's kind of like it's always been, only different."

"Did we go into space?" I said. "Have we colonised the moon, and Mars?"

"Oh, no," he said. Then he suddenly brightened up, as though he'd just thought of something that he thought would please me. "But we do have a space station," he said.

"A space station?"

"Sure. In orbit."

"What does it do?"

"I don't know. Floats there?"

"Is there world peace?" I said. "Is there a world government?"

"No, sorry. It never really worked out that way, you know."

"Do you have overpopulation?"

"Sure, I guess. It's not so bad. We do have global warming, though."

"What's that?"

He shrugged. "Burning too many fossil fuels and that," he said.

"You'll never make a good science fiction writer," I told him. "You make it all sound so dull and commonplace."

"We do have robots though!" he said, eager to please.

"Really? Do they look just like people, and serve everyone in their homes?"

"Oh, no, it's not like that—" I somehow knew that was what he was going to say. "They just build things, in automated factories. Cars and, you know. Other machines."

I was getting bored talking to him. "Have you ever met Robert Heinlein?" I said.

"Heinlein? But he's famous!"

I didn't like the way he said it—like Heinlein was going to be a bigger deal than me. "Let me introduce you," I said, smiling. I turned from him for a moment, calling out, "Bob, Bob! Come over here!"

"What?" Heinlein said irritably, ambling over with a drink in his hand.

"I wanted you to meet someone," I said, turning back to my unexpected companion—only now there was no sign of him.

He'd disappeared.

"Very funny, Gene," Heinlein said.

"I swear he was here just a minute ago. Damnedest thing. Claimed he was a time-traveller. From the future."

Heinlein snorted. Then he said, "You should write a book like that."

1943

I joined up after Pearl Harbor. Of course I signed up. Asimov was in the Philadelphia Navy Yard—the kid idolised me just like Campbell did. Heinlein joined him there, too. I did my basic training in Hawaii. I still wrote, dashing off a story here and there to Campbell when I could, and happily collecting checks. I became conscious of the yachts that thronged the piers, and I determined that one day I would have not just one, but an entire fleet of them. I didn't know how. But I knew I could do anything, be anything.

I just had to get through the war.

28.

1944

I flew to Espiritu Santo from Hawaii on a Catalina PBY—a flying boat. "Indian Joe" Bauer piloted the plane. They later shot him down over Guadalcanal and later still named an airport after him. He'd shot down plenty of planes in the war before they finally got him. The hours passed. I tried to doze, read a battered issue of *Astounding Science Fiction*, with part of a space serial by E. E. "Doc" Smith, and one of my own, "The Devourers," which I had knocked out earlier in the year. We briefly came under attack from Babs, Japanese single-engine monoplanes, but the Catalina's gunner soon scared them off. In the ocean below I spotted a whale, rising momentarily to the surface, blowing out a jet of salt water before the immense, dark bulk was again submerged. At last, in the middle of all that water, islands came into view. They were mountainous, covered in an impregnable canopy of green, surrounded by dazzling white sand and coral reefs. We flew over the open peak of a volcano rising from deep within the ocean, its crater a lake of steaming water: from high above it appeared like a vast blue eye staring upwards. Beyond that came the island of Espiritu Santo, like a small continent, and buildings came into view, a wharf, several navy ships, smaller boats, and three other PBYs bobbing in a bay. We landed in the water and were rowed ashore in native canoes.

Luganville had been a small, sleepy colonial town. Once South Pacific Command, however, decided in their infinite wisdom that these islands would best serve the war effort as an advance base, our ships turned up one day, like the ghost ships which the Ni-Vanuatu believed carried the souls of their dead far away. They sailed into harbour, taking over the abandoned colonial infrastructure of the French, and began to construct the base. In the time I was there, three airfields had been erected and the waves of planes coming and going to and from the battles over the Solomons to the northwest were unceasing. Many of the planes crashed on takeoff and many others crashed enroute, and to this day you can find the remnants of old fighters buried deep within the evergreen forests. Shortly after arriving I fell ill with malaria and for several days was haunted by strange dreams in which I was being eaten by giant insects. I woke up sweating, in turns hot and cold under the mosquito net. It rained hot, big wet drops down from the clouded sky, and I felt a strange relief at not being able to see the stars.

In the event I was seconded to III Island Command's coast-watching operation. We were delivered up to the islands by the Echo, a converted civilian lumber schooner. There was Maguire on Tongoa, and two men to keep Ruby Boye company on Van-ikoro. There were groups off to Epi, Malekula, Aurora, all the lonely islands of the reach. And then there was Hawthorn for Vanua Lava, Hawthorn with Tom, and Billy, and myself.

Native porters helped carry our equipment from Sola. It was a desolate coconut plantation, hastily abandoned by its French overseer when war broke out. Broken black rocks marked the end of the bay, and mangrove swamps extended inland until one reached the jutting pier. A volcanic peak, surrounded by steam and clouds. Thunder, echoing and multiplying across the bay. Tiny sand crabs ran away as we stepped on land. The natives carried our radio and portable generator, fifty gallons of fuel and ninety days' worth of tinned food. We were armed with M-1 rifles and one Browning automatic. The uniforms clung to our bodies with sweat. The island was mountainous, sparsely populated. The coconut trees gave way to natangura and nangae, banyan and narafika. In my time there I learned to recognise them all, the hard nuts of the nangae and the small, sweet fruit of the narafika trees, and the tall, majestic banyans that marked the meeting place of a village, called a nasara. We learned, too, to avoid the poisonous nangalat, to seek, deep in the bush, the small, curious fungus that glowed in the dark, to hunt for mussels and naora on rare excursions to the beach at Sanara. We quickly came to rely on our native guides, to supplement our meals with local taro, manioc, fish, papaya, and we learned to hunt for the cores of fermented coconuts lying on the forest floor, to dig out their soft, spongy insides, a delicacy I would miss in the years to come.

Quickly we established base camp, high on the hill called Leserser. From there we could see as far as the reaches of the Solomon Islands. Towering in the distance was Bligh's Island, Ureparapara, a malevolent broken volcano rising out of the sea. Beyond it was the chain of low-lying Torres Islands and beyond those, the Santa Cruz Islands of the Solomons.

Everywhere there was the deep blue sky and the endless sea, and the islands rising like green-backed turtles. Volcanoes steamed in every direction and overhead the planes flew constantly, back and forth, ours and theirs. We looked out for Japanese submarines, the flash of light rising out of the ocean. Once, one had wandered into the channel between Vanua Lava and Gaua. We radioed it in and a squadron was sent from Santo. As the submarine rose the bombers attacked. The explosions wrecked the hull, and the sailors and their cargo, broken, were lifted out of the metal womb and cast adrift in the sea. For weeks later, debris would wash ashore at Sanara, the gas-bloated corpses of the Japanese men, and with them bottles, tins, machinery and broken crates, and shoes. The shoes were the most valued by the locals. We did six-hour shifts up on the tree, six hours of watching for enemy movement, six hours at a time with nothing but the sun or the stars for company. I grew to hate the stars.

When I could, I would sneak down to the village. Mosina sat in the bush, close to a perfect white sand beach, on the other side of the bay from Sola. Its shore faced out to Gaua and Espiritu Santo. The ocean waters were deep and clear there, and one could catch fish with bare hands, standing chest-high in the water. I drank kava with the men, a drink made of the roots of a plant that looks like a tangled beard. I listened to their stories. Then, too, there was a girl in the village, and I had never been shy of a girl or an opinion. I hated the nights, the way the Milky Way dominated the sky, the way it stretched across from one horizon to the other, like a fault line in the sky made up of stars. The stars were so thick in the arms of the galaxy that they looked like fine dust, and crossing the band of light I would often see a black rift between the stars, running from Cygnus to Sagittarius. It was around that time, too, that I fell ill again, and as I lay retching and shivering under the stars, savaged by mosquitoes, I began to see the true shape of all things, and the outline of a woman, young and yet old, travelling across space in the light of old stars.

1945

In my dreams, more and more, I could see faces. They were everywhere in the bush: peering at me from the interplay of leaves and shadows, from the formation of bark, from the fall of moonlight on machine guns. I woke up shivering within the dream. The night was hot, stuffy. The air was still. Mosquitoes buzzed in the undergrowth. Black ants crawled single file along a natangura root. The air smelled of mulch, of rotting leaves and stagnant water, and of the ocean in the distance. Corporal Hawthorn was asleep. After six months in the bush I knew his face as intimately as my own. Mine, on the other hand, had become a stranger's. When I caught glimpse of myself, unexpectedly, a reflection in glass or a body of water, I was startled anew by this unknown man, this doppelganger. I wore a thick black beard and my eyes were sunk into my face, and I was covered in bites. We moved jerkily, we men, scratching constantly. Bill was up on the tree, watching. We still did six-hour shifts, taking turns. Tom Carroll was on the radio. I heard snatches of static, reports from the control tower at Santo, retorts from squadron planes returning from the Solomons. There were four of us in the bush.

I lit a cigarette, drew in the smoke greedily. The generator hummed nearby. Faces stared at me from the undergrowth.

After six months here I was used to their presence. Sometimes they resembled small men with mottled, thick beards, like the tangled roots of the kava plant. The local people called them uturgurgur or, in pidgin, ol olfala blong bus, the old men of the forest. We were invaders into their land. Their villages were said to be set in the roots of great nambanga trees. I knew they were watching. They dogged our steps wherever we went, yet melted into the shadows as though they never existed when I challenged them.

It was always twilight under the canopy of trees. "Hartley, you're up next," Corporal Hawthorn said, without opening his eyes.

"Sir, yes sir," I said, with no enthusiasm. I put out the cigarette and began to climb the tree. I did not know the native name for it. It jutted out of the canopy, hundreds of years old, patient, alive. We had hammered foot- and hand-holds into it and built an observation deck at the top. I climbed. The forest stretched around me. I pulled and rose, hand, foot, step by step rising high and higher. At last I breached the canopy of the trees.

Below me, the South Pacific Ocean stretched in all directions. Silver moonlight cast an eerie glow over the volcano. The primordial forest fell away from me, down the hill and all across the island. Only on the shore it was finally stopped, held back, and there I could see the small human settlements of Sola and Mosina and Vureas Bay. Thin reeds of smoke rose out of the settlements, and thick hot fog rose out of the volcano. I could hear no birds. The silence was profound. Beyond the island I could see other islands in the distance, dark green turtle shells floating in the dark blue sea. At last I looked up, but the top of the tree and the coastwatching station were gone, and in their place were the stars.

The sky was a black chasm and stars were painted on it. They shone down, cold and bright. I felt fear grip me. I held on to the wood. These were not the stars seen from Earth, but an alien view, seen from an impossible distance. There were too many stars. As I watched they moved, pulled by an invisible, dark force. There were spirals of stars, entire galaxies, rotating in the sky above me, drawn towards a central, all-encompassing darkness.

29.

1948

After the war I bummed around California for a while. I took a gig writing B-pictures for Rathvon at RKO. The only one that ever got made was *Lone Star Vigilantes*, a cowboy picture with Bob Steele, which tells you all you need to know. I was still knocking out stories for John W. Campbell, and occasionally hung out with the other pulpsters on the West Coast. Like me, Robert Heinlein had come out of the war and was writing for *Astounding*, quite successfully. He also made the break out of the science fiction ghetto into the "slicks," selling a story to the *Saturday Evening Post*. I envied him that. I wanted more than I had, more than anyone had. The shadows of the war were dormant for a time. I'd meet Heinlein for drinks every now and then and we'd shoot the breeze, talking wordage and cents.

"You know," he said to me, quite drunk one time, "if you really want to make a million bucks, Gene, you should start your own religion." And he laughed. Soon after that he divorced Leslyn and married Virginia and they moved to

Colorado, and I didn't see much of him anymore.

My own marriage had collapsed long before that. I had married young and I liked women too much to remain married. Susie stayed in Montana with the children. I missed Eugene, Jr. I remembered holding him in my hands when he was born, how small he was, how helpless. I marvelled that this tiny creature could be my son, a part of me, yet its own, unknown creature. He was doing well, as was his sister, and I sent money over to Susie when I could, which wasn't often. I'd spend days in my studio apartment, banging away on the typewriter: spaceships and aliens, and heroes who could save the world. Then I'd amble blinking into the late afternoon's light. I could get drunk on California sunsets. At dusk on the beach the tall tanned girls passed, as cool and inviting as highballs. I went to parties at my old pal Jack Parsons' house. There was always someone to talk to there, from rocket scientists to science fiction fans to strange little occultists who worshipped Crowley, and there were always girls, and they helped me forget the war and forget the New Hebrides, those goddamned islands, peaking out of the endless ocean like the bright glittering scales of a vast sea serpent. I remembered the volcano, and at night we'd see strange lights on Surevuvu, the hill which the locals called the place of the dead. There had been a girl in the village of Mosina, as I mentioned, and it's possible I got her pregnant.

But then the war ended and I left. And there were always other girls.

Sometime in '48, "Doc" Lowndes organised a get-together, what the fans were beginning to call a convention. It was at the Park View Manor, a one-day event, which they decided to call a "Westercon," and I went along as one of the speakers. That kid,

Bradbury, was there, who was already writing for *Astounding*, and the Canadian, A. E. Van Vogt. He'd moved to California by that time and was a prolific pulpster, as well-known as I was. Around seventy or eighty people attended that day, and they wandered about bright-eyed with optimism—about the future, about the world. The war had ended. America was prosperous, powerful, youthful, and great. Everything was possible. We were already building rockets that could one day reach the stars. The atom bomb had been deployed and signalled the end of the war. You have to understand—we were more than writers, we were prophets of a new age. We could see the future, we could imagine it and give it shape. Later, Van Vogt and I got roaringly drunk at some nameless beach-front bar that never seemed to close. He worshipped me a little, I think. All his stories were about supermen, new mental systems that gave their initiates powers beyond imagining. Two years earlier he'd published a novel, *Slan*, about these supermen. The science fiction fans adored it. They saw the hunted, persecuted slans as embodiments of themselves. It didn't make much more sense than anything else but it did get me to thinking, later. You have to understand that back then we were all looking for something, if only something to believe in. As for Van Vogt, I think he actually believed his own stories. He used to ask his wife to wake him up every ninety minutes when he slept, just so that he could record his dreams, which he then used for his writing.

"What are you going to do?" he asked me, that night, after too many tequilas.

"What do you mean?"

"You're not one of us," he said without rancour. "Not really, Gene. Sometimes I think you're only writing science fiction because it's easy for you and it's better than work."

"But it is easy for me," I said. "And it sure as hell beats working for a living, Van."

He smiled at that, but a little sadly. He wasn't much of a drinker at the best of times, and his eyes had a glazed look, like submerged amber.

"Me," he said, "I just want to write. That's what I do, Gene. I'm a writer. A pulp writer, maybe, but a writer. That's all I've ever wanted to do. What I'm asking you is, what do *you* want to do with the rest of your life?"

I shrugged, a little discomfited. I lit a cigarette. The waves crashed against the shore gently, and a full moon hovered over the dark water. Somewhere in the distance a ship was edging to land. A redhead on a stool by the bar turned and gave me a smile that held a world of promises.

"Bum around," I said. "See the world, maybe. Get laid."

"You're better than that," he said. "You could be greater than all of us, Gene, if you only let yourself be free."

"I don't know what that means, Van," I said, with an irritation I didn't want to show. Sooner or later with those true believers, you had to be subjected to a lecture. I'd lost count of the times I'd had to listen to people telling me all about telepathy, or lizard men, or lunar colonies. Heinlein always went on in praise of nudism. I didn't have the heart to tell him no one wanted to see his dick flopping about, thank you all the same.

"I don't know," Van Vogt said. "I just feel like you're running from something."

"We're all running from something," I said.

"Maybe I'm wrong," he said. His face looked green and he said, "I don't feel too well."

"Come on," I said. I put my arm under him and helped him to his feet. He staggered outside and was sick on the sand. I watched him, with the smoke of my cigarette framing the scene.

"Better?" I said.

He wiped his mouth with the back of his hand. "Listen," he said. "If I'm wrong, well, I've been wrong before. But if I'm right, Gene, if you find what it is you're looking for, if you find your truth and it's a truth worth sharing, then know that I'll be here, and I'll be ready to listen."

He meant only that he wanted someone else to front his mad beliefs: about the superiority of Man and the right to bear arms, the hidden powers we could have if only we could somehow unlock our own minds, how we could rule the world, the galaxy. John W. Campbell loved him for a reason.

But I was not a Van Vogt. I did not know what I believed, not then, but I was not so sure we were superior, God's chosen ones. I wasn't sure what we were, if we were anything at all. All I knew was what I thought I saw, in the bush, on Leserser, during that long, dark year of silence in the South Pacific. All I knew was that I felt the press of stars overhead, and they were cold, and bright, and indifferent. "Come on, Van," I said, and helped him walk back inside, "I'll call you a cab."

Later, the redheaded girl came over and sat with me, and we went back to her place. In the night I woke up, covered in sweat, my heart hammering in my chest like a prisoner pleading to be let out. The moon floated outside the window. The girl lay sleeping beside me, her arm draped across a pillow. I lit a cigarette and watched the bright moon, and tried not to look to either side, where I knew the shadows whispered.

1952

Parsons died in an explosion. I would rather not think about it. There were all kinds of stories.

I took his boat. I sailed it to Mexico.

1953

Letter from John W. Campbell to Isaac Asimov, March 17, 1953

Dear Isaac,

Einstein—who is one of your people, of course—ushered in a new way of thinking about the properties of space with his seminal equations, which there is no denying, yet he lacked the science fiction writers' powers of what I call "disciplined imagination." I mention this as Eugene Hartley has unexpectedly been in touch with me recently. He is holed up somewhere in Mexico, with, as he says in his letter, "Nothing but my trusty old typewriter, a bottle of bourbon and some delightful female company"—Hartley in a nutshell, as I'm sure you'll agree!

I know you have always looked up to him somewhat. I had always looked upon him as a promising—indeed, brilliant—author in our field, but I am beginning to find his recent *communiqué* troubling. He had enclosed a story, "Lunar Messiah," with the request that, should I accept it (which, he wrote, he sincerely hopes that I do!) to forward the check with all haste to his *poste restante* address. I get the sense he is, as usual, low on money. The story is more than adequate, and the readers always look forward to a new Hartley story. I had sent back the check with due haste, with a note to the effect that I hope he uses the money for some fresh groceries.

Fresh vegetables, as I'm sure you'll agree, Isaac, are an important source of nutrients, while being naturally low in fat. Aldous Huxley, I am told, is a vegetarian. So was George Bernard Shaw. It occurs to me that many people choose the path of vegetarianism due to some misplaced aversion to the consumption of sentient life. Yet what is sentience? Can a cow or a pig truly be called "sentient"? It raises interesting questions. For instance—here is an idea for a story for you, Ike—what if plants, too, were sentient? It occurs to me that there is much room in the idea of experimenting with telepathy not with other human beings but with trees or flowers. An Indian scientist, by the name of Chandra Bose, conducted just such experiments in the turn of the century. I am told he also wrote science fiction, which I find hard to credit. The mind of the Indian is a superstitious place and they are generally incapable of logic, though some, I'll grant you, are certainly bright enough. They had let themselves be lorded over by the British, who treat them rather like the children that they are. It is indeed the duty of our higher civilization to educate and "uplift" (if I may be so bold as to coin a term!) the more backwards people of this planet.

Yet I believe the idea of communicating with plants is not without merit, and have indeed discussed just such a research project with a young fellow, by the name of Backster, who currently works for our Central Intelligence Agency. He was much captivated by the theories I espoused, and enthusiastically assured me that he intends to follow up on my ideas with practical research. I have no doubt he would be able to prove what I had merely conjectured!

Well, we were speaking of sentience, and Einstein, which in a roundabout way is what Hartley's letter was about. He has devised, he says, some sort of non-planetary system, based on Einstein's equations and the research of a fellow by the name of Schwarzschild, who I am sure you are familiar with. It concerns certain stars which, when they die, collapse into a gravitational point so strong that it pulls to it not only matter but even light itself. Hartley suggests the name "Lode Stars" for such hypothetical systems, from Shakespeare, of all people—"Your eyes are lodestars"—in *A Midsummer's Night's Dream*, as I am sure you know (I well remember how fond you are of your Shakespeare, Ike!). Frankly, it seems a little nonsensical to me, but Hartley seems dead set on writing something set in such a system, and the potential applications truly are fascinating. However, he is not his usual rational self, but has ascribed all manner of mystical nonsense to these "lode stars." Do you know what happened to him in California? I fear it may have affected the poor man's mind. Meanwhile, thank you for sending the rewritten version of your latest story. I will be glad to publish "Belief" in the October issue. It occurs to me that were levitation proven to be workable, the practical applications would be tremendous. However, as your story so aptly concludes, the fact that we do not understand is not the issue, but that we must try to understand. Kelly Freas will be doing the cover, which I think you'll like. Kay has cut you a check, which is in the post.

Regards, John

Letter from Jack Kerouac to Allen Ginsberg, April 12, 1953

. . . and the girl said "Screw you, gringo!" to Neal with wounded dignity and staggered from there,

the bottle of wine still in her hand
and her head held high and proud
against the reddening skies. I felt
a great love and affection and desire
intermingled for her but she walked
away from us forever, and I could
taste the sadness in my gums and
wanted to wash it with wine. Then
Hartley said, "You want to hear
something amazing?" This Hartley was
an American washed up on this alien
shore; we'd met him that afternoon
as we were trailing a little boy
who promised us girls, and tea to
smoke. It had been a hot afternoon
and the kid took us to this shack on
the edge of the town where all the
girls were asleep in the heat, drunk
on it, and the only man there and
awake was this Hartley, who greeted
us like long-lost souls.

Neal had a girl in his lap and he
was making her laugh and she wrig-
gled. We were holed up somewhere
south of the border and the sun was
setting and the sky was red and then
it turned black and the stars came
out. "You think you know stars?"
Hartley said, waving a copy of some
pulp magazine. It had a sort of
spaceship on the cover. "I like you,

Jack, but I'm the greatest fucking writer in this whole fucking world if not the next and more than that, I know the truth, I've finally figured it out."

Neal wasn't listening, he was busy with his girl, but I was still filled with all the sadness of my true love's parting and I never even knew her name. I needed to get laid but I had time and there were other girls. Candles burned around the room and the roof was open to the sky. Hartley grabbed me in a bear hug and wrestled me to the floor as the whores watched, laughing. "Stop struggling," he said, "and lie down and look at the stars and have a taste of this."

He pushed a giant marijuana cigarette into my hand and lit it; it took him five matches but he finally got a light going and when he touched it to the tip of the bomber the smoke roared in my lungs and the world tilted sideways and was right again. "Look at them," he said. His breath was hot and heavy on my face. "*Look* at them!"

We lay side by side in easy companionship and passed the bomber to each other like lovers exchanging a kiss. There were not many lights in that town and the sky was black and clear and there was no moon. The stars came out then, spinning out of the primordial matter of the universe into existence overhead, until first the one tentacle and then another appeared and the whole glorious beautiful galaxy in which we find ourselves materialised into being, like wisps of smoke at first and then thickening and growing bright and real and incontrovertible and Hartley said, "Do you *see*? Do you *see*, Jack?" and my breath escaped me like a spirit, aching to rise into that whole infinite impossible creation.

"Who *made* this?" I said, and he leaned over me, his eyes as big as moons, and said, "God."

We both burst out laughing, together, giggling like little girls there on the dirt floor of that nameless brothel with the Mexican whores watching us and Neal grunting in a back room loud through the thin walls. I loved to hear him fuck. He was never more beautiful or more true.

"God?" I said. "How do you know God, Hartley?"

"I don't," he said. "But I will, and so will you. Don't you get it, Jack? We are all *information*!" It was getting hard to listen because of the tea and I was sure I could feel the Earth actually spinning and riding through space around the sun and rushing too as the galaxy spun and took us on a journey to who knew where. I wanted to close my eyes and go for the ride but Hartley was still talking, he hadn't stopped talking since we'd got there in the early afternoon, I didn't think he'd spoken to anyone in months unless it was to the girls to pay them.

"Information," I mumbled. Neal was still going at it beyond the wall.

"Look at all those stars!" Hartley said. "And all of them moving, and we with them. Spinning and spinning around a great black nothingness, a place where the laws of space and time break down. Einstein called it a singularity, but he'd not worked out the implications. It's right there, in the center of the galaxy! A big, black . . . *hole* in the world, pulling us all, stars, planets, comets, life

and people. You and me." He sank
back to the ground, exhausted. Two
girls came and sat on either side of
him and just watched him with big
brown eyes.

"God's not here," he said, quietly.
"God's not here, Sal. But he's
watching."

In the morning he was gone like
he'd never been. He'd left a disconcerting note, though:

See you in a few billion years

Letter from John W. Campbell to Eugene Hartley, May 2, 1953

Dear Gene,

I must express some concern with
your latest submission. I note that
your prose has become more wild of
late. Have you been reading C. L.
Moore? This isn't science, this is
science *fantasy*—thieves' planets and
crumbling temples, mysterious alien
mafiosi—please! There is a good idea
buried somewhere within this tale
but for the life of me I am having
trouble comprehending it.

Take your "lode stars"—exactly what
scientists have you been speaking

to? I've gone so far as to write to Clarke—he is still in London, yet speaks of emigrating somewhere warm to pursue his diving—Ceylon, perhaps. He confirms that Einstein's theory of general relativity does allow for something like a "black hole," though he finds most of your subsequent ideas as to their nature rather fanciful. The readers, no doubt, would lap this up—were it served to them in *Thrilling Wonder Stories* or *Galaxy*! I expect rather more here at *Astounding*.

Moreover, Gene, the story is not even complete! Clearly you are working on something larger than a short story here—a novella, maybe even a novel? Perhaps, were it completed, we could serialise it, but consider this: the readers of *Astounding* are men of science—they are problem-solvers! Your characters so far do nothing but run around like hysterical women! What is worse, you seem to suggest the two "companions" may be Sapphic, and this really isn't acceptable, Gene, no matter how liberal you think yourself—it is not that I, personally, take exception to the sisterhood of the comfortable shoes, but the readers, Gene! The readers would never stand for it. What else would you have them do, kiss, in some act of cosmic perversion? What your story lacks is a hero, an Earthman who could think logically and scientifically of the issues you raise. This absent father of whom we keep hearing so much, for instance. Write me *his* story, and I'd buy it!

And consider: who is this "God" you keep bringing up? If the universe is an experiment created by these alien beings, then what is its purpose?

I did, however, enjoy the passing reference to a "Tweel"—poor Stan Weinbaum! I never got to publish "A Martian Odyssey," which appeared elsewhere, but I did publish several of his other tales before he succumbed to that awful lung cancer at such an untimely young age, and I am sure he would have raised a chuckle at your reference to his story.

Thank you for the regards to Dona but, as I must have written to you previously, we had got divorced, and I am now married to Peg. She is a delightful girl and it is for the best, but it does mean it has been too long since I last saw you. I do hope you come back soon to New York. Meanwhile, finish this story! Make it work!

Regards,
John

Letter from Robert Heinlein to Eugene Hartley, June 30, 1953

Dear Gene,
  Good, as always, to hear from you on your travails. I do feel calling poor Campbell an SOB is a little unwarranted—he certainly has his tics and foibles as an editor, and ones we know all too well—why not just write him the sort of story he likes to pay for? Give him a competent man and an unsolvable mystery, then solve it—this is the sort of thing you could do in your sleep. I myself, I feel, will soon outgrow him—the money's in books now, novels—I have been writing "juveniles" for a while now and I believe that's where the money is, unless you do as you keep threatening to, and indeed start

your own religion! Remember Ike Asimov when you told him that, that one night at Campbell's place? The look on the kid's face was priceless.

Ginny and I are well, and are busy designing our own model house of the future here in Colorado—it will have an entirely controlled indoor temperature (like a miniature weather machine!) and a central radio and record player wired to speakers scattered throughout the house, even a working office in the kitchen for Ginny, so that she can type and answer the phone while doing the cooking. In many ways it is the ideal home for us, and I hope it will soon be finished.

What *are* you doing in Mexico? I'm attaching a postal order for some $200 with this letter. Us writers must look out for each other—no one else will, after all. Look after yourself, Gene, and come back to the old U.S. of A. soon—next year's Worldcon is in Chicago, and old Hugo "The Rat" Gernsback is the guest of honor! Near a thousand people have registered, if you can believe it. These things seem to be getting bigger every year—soon everyone, it seems, will be into science fiction.

Take care, Gene, and whatever happens, keep writing—with just a typewriter, men like you and me can change the world.

Bob

Letter from L. Sprague de Camp to Robert A. Heinlein, April 25, 1954

Dear Bob,

It sounds to me like Gene is putting on his old "Poor Wounded Soldier" racket once again—though as far as I know he spent the majority of the war holed up on some South Pacific island paradise! He's written to me too, and recently, asking for money, but I do not have your largesse of heart—nor indeed your sizeable pockets.

For what it's worth, I do like Gene—he can be an entertaining, if often overbearing, dinner companion, and his tall tales can be amusing, so long as he does not repeat them excessively. I have never understood the obvious attraction he exerts on impressionable young women, but there is no denying it either, and I have no doubt at this very moment he is on the lookout for an attractive woman to finance him for a time. How many girls can one screw in a lifetime, anyway? I dare say he would be reincarnated as a rabbit in his next life.

He is a good if unexceptional writer, I find, and the ideas you mention—this cosmic "searching for God" stuff—frankly sounds like just another one of his cons. He can be charming—when he wants something from you. It sounds like so far Campbell has been immune to his mysticism, but don't be fooled—you know Campbell's enthusiasms, and I suspect it won't be long before Gene's won him over with this non-sense. I fear the money you sent him was ill spent.

My regards to Ginny—Catherine and I are well, and looking forward to seeing you both soon—when will you swing by the East Coast again?

Yours, etc.,
Sprague

30.

1955

When I returned from Mexico I went back to New York for a time. I visited the White Horse Tavern, but the old pulpsters were no longer there—Dent, Gibson, the ones I'd used to look up to, back when I was a little kid. They'd written *Doc Savage* and *The Shadow*, typing furiously, millions of words, galaxies of words. I had almost no money. I was holed up at the Chelsea but it was full of *poseurs*. I slept fitfully. The nightmares had followed me from Mexico. The air in my room was sluggish and clammy. In my dreams eyes like chitinous insects bore into me, hungry teeth ringing their corneas. Then they changed, abruptly, and it was a memory I was walking through.

In my dream I was back in Jack Parsons' huge, shambling mansion in Pasadena. Palm trees bent in the high wind outside. It was night and the stars were out. I was in a dark corridor. Ahead of me I saw a sliver of light under the door. I heard chanting, low and menacing. I edged along the dark corridor. The chanting grew louder. I pushed the door half-open, and saw, in the dark room beyond, three figures, two in black robes, one naked on an altar. Of the two men in the robes one was chanting. The other was naked underneath the robe and he approached the woman on the altar with his wand raised.

"Oh circle of stars," chanted the priest, who I knew to be Parsons. "Whereof our Father is but the younger brother, marvel beyond imagination, soul of infinite space!"

The woman writhed on the altar. Her voice was melodious and urgent. "But to love me is better than all things," she replied. "Put on the wings and arouse the coiled splendour within you. Come unto me, to me!"

The disrobed man advanced on her and sank into her flesh, losing himself between her parted legs. I did not need to look at his face to know him, for I was him, and he was me. We had enacted this ritual just before poor Parsons' death, my flight to Mexico.

Betty had come with me, but we shortly thereafter separated.

"Glory unto the Scarlet Woman, Babalon, the Mother of Abominations, that rideth upon the Beast!" cried Parsons. The wind screamed outside and then the roof was torn off and the cold bright stars shone down, swirling round a huge black emptiness. The air filled with the smell of sex and Betty's cries and my doppelganger's grunts and Parsons' fevered intonation. A smell like cordite filled the air.

I stared into the blackness above. I realised that the darkness was in fact the door to a massive building, and I was standing outside it; the sky was grey and it was cold and the air smelled of glue and paper and the ground shook as though there was an earthquake. Above the great doors was a frowning owl above a double S, and the address 79 Seventh Avenue.

This was a more recent memory: only the week before I had gone to the Smith & Street Publications offices, the manuscript, like a talisman of protection, in its leather case under my arm.

I pushed the doors open and went inside, where the smell of glue intensified and the ground shook continuously, as though many feet were marching in formation behind the walls. The stooped receptionist welcomed me in, then led me down endless corridors, through vast rooms where giant presses hummed and burped and stomped, churning out endless rolls of pulp paper, which lay all about the place in piles higher than my head. At last she took me to an ancient elevator and I pulled the ancient rope to rise. It ascended, creaking through the boom of the printing presses until I pulled on the rope again for it to stop. Here through corridors and offices, the sound of the printing presses and their thrum still felt, but fainter, and I thought I was not even in the same building anymore, but another, adjoining it. I came at last to a tiny office, where a tall, handsome man sat behind a desk laden with papers. He inserted a Camel cigarette into a holder and lit it, and drew the smoke and blew it into the already-toxic air.

"Hello, Eugene," he said, amiably. It was my old-time editor at *Astounding*, John W. Campbell.

"John," I said. I slammed the thick bundle of the manuscript on his desk. "You must read this! It will change the course of history."

"Do you believe the earth is hollow?" Campbell said. He always went on like that. The man was a first-class bore, but always mailed my checks on time. "This fellow Shaver is very convincing on that score. He claims thousands of people every year are abducted by the hidden denizens of the subterranean world, to work as slaves."

"No!" I said. "I do not believe that nonsense, John." I was giddy with urgency. They were close; shadows whispered to me from the corners of the office. I gestured at my manuscript beseechingly.

"Do you believe in UFOs?" he said. "Only, Kenneth Arnold is very convincing about his sighting of what appeared to be alien craft in the sky near Mount Rainier."

"No," I said. It was hot inside his office and I felt as though black ants were crawling all over me, the way they had in the bush, in the Pacific during the war. I wanted to scratch and scratch and scratch.

"Do you believe in the Dean Drive?" he said. "Only, Lomer Dean is very convincing in his demonstration of a reactionless drive, which seems to prove Newton's Laws were wrong all along."

I stared at him in horror.

"No!" I screamed. "I do not believe in UFOs, I do not believe in the Dean Drive, I do not believe in the Hollow Earth, or Bigfoot, or the Jewish Conspiracy, or the fucking Loch Ness Monster, John! I believe in the immutable laws of physics; I believe the universe was created; that it is a universe fine-tuned to evolve life; and that someone, John, or some thing is watching it all, hidden from us in the Ur-universe beyond. They are watching us, Don! Now read my goddamned manuscript!"

"I don't know how to tell you this, Eugene," John Campbell said, "but you sound like a total lunatic."

1962

Letter from Alfred Bester to Frederik Pohl, August 2, 1962

I submitted a story to Campbell the other day, and to my surprise he telephoned me, demanding I come see him in his office. I had never met the man, and had no desire to ever visit New Jersey—I mean, I work on Madison Avenue, for chrissake. I know the networks, executives, admen.

But I have to meet him, right? So I go to New Jersey.

Campbell's a veritable giant, sitting hunched up in this tiny office in the middle of this huge, awful printing press somewhere in deepest darkest Jersey. He lights up a cigarette and stares at me through the thick cloud of smoke. All the while the machines are thumping through the walls and the floor, it feels like one is in some hostile womb of some sort.

"Read this," he says to me. He thrusts a galley proof into my hands. *Lode Stars*, by Eugene Hartley, that friend of yours.

"Hartley?" I say. "I thought he

was dead."

"Dead?" Campbell says, and his eyes glitter oddly. "Dead, well, that's one way to put it. We're all dead, if you think far enough ahead, Alfie."

There's a lot of pages there. I tell him that. "Gee, Mr. Campbell. Can I take them home with me?"

He shakes his head. "It's too important," he says. "I want you to read it now, while your mind's fresh. This is going to change the world."

I take a look. It's all rousing stuff, though when I try to think back on it the details seem to escape me. Something about a girl, Delia, walking along the circumference of the world. . . .

Odd stuff indeed.

"Well?" Campbell demands, after a while. I raise my head. "Well, what?" I say.

"Well, what do you *think*?" he cries. "Will he win the Nobel?"

"For literature?"

"For *peace*," he says.

"Oh, sure," I say. "Why?"

"Because this could end war. This could revolutionize everything. Our place in the cosmos! Our manifest destiny!"

"Sure, Mr. Campbell," I say. "That's right."

"Come on, let's have lunch," he tells me. He takes me down to this tacky little lunchroom. We sit down. I have a liverwurst sandwich on rye and a Coke.

"Think forward!" he says.

"Yes, Mr. Campbell."

"You, me, Gene, we're all possibly dead already."

"Sure, Mr. Campbell."

"This world could be an illusion. A reconstruction. Don't you see?"

"Yes, Mr. Campbell."

"You don't see," he says, accusingly. "You're blocking it. Try to remember your death!"

"Mr. Campbell, I can't remember what hasn't happened yet," I tell him.

"Think! Remember forward!"

I'm shaking, trying not to laugh.

"Remember forward, Alfie!"

"You're right," I finally tell him. "I'm trying, but it's too hard. It's too painful for me, Mr. Campbell!"

"I knew it," he says. He sits back with satisfaction. "I could see you shaking."

Fred—what an awful man! A great

editor, but he's declining fast, chasing one bizarre belief after another. Mark my words, between him and Hartley, only one ego could eventually survive this unholy union.

Note from Dorothea Smith to John W. Campbell, March 21, 1965

Dear Mr. Campbell,

As communicated previously several times already, Mr. Hartley is at the moment on a long lecture tour of Europe and will not be available in the near future. In the interest of expediency, pleased refrain from further *communiqués*, as they shall go unanswered.

Regretfully,
Yrs. etc.,
Dorothea Smith, CEO
Lode Stars, Inc.

31.

1966

Letter from Judith Merril to Virginia Kidd, 30 May 1966

Dear Kidd,

The weather here in London is intermittently warm, with bouts of rain that never lash so much as drizzle. Will there ever be a summer? Or proper rain? The kid and I are staying in a tiny bedsit in Notting Hill, near Mike Moorcock and his wife, who live in a charming little flat, and there is always so much going on. There is much of an uproar over Mike's editing of *New Worlds* and the movement they're now calling the New Wave, led by Jim Ballard, who I've met several times now. Other Americans are always floating around—Chip Delany popped up on his way to the continent, Tom Disch is constantly about, everyone's sleeping with everyone else, and I'm busy working on that anthology I promised David Grinnell at Ace.

But the real news isn't the New Wave, or even the new Beatles album—it's Eugene Hartley and his Lode Star Kids.

Remember Gene? The cocky young pulpster who was always palling around with Heinlein back in the day? Well, he ain't so young anymore (but then, who of us is?) and he's not in the pulp business either, but he sure is still cocky. He's swept into town last week, apparently, and there's been no end of fuss about it in the papers, what with his doomsday church or whatever it is, though he says he's here just to give a lecture tour. But the Brits have gone mad for him, and he's surrounded by young girls with flowers in their hair wherever he goes. He popped into Mike's flat unexpectedly the other night, swanning into the room as though he already owned it, expecting everyone to be full of awe, I suppose. Some of the Young

Turks tried to shoot him down but he charmed them, sure enough. Listening to him, you'd think he'd single-handedly ushered in science fiction's Golden Age, while wrestling bears and winning World War Two in the bargain. I am not even sure he remembered me, and he didn't stay long, in any case—he had a function to go to in Kensington, he said, a *soiree* hosted by the duke of something-or-other.

Truthfully, though, Kidd? There was something in his eyes I didn't much like, and I don't think he did either. I noticed him catching his reflection, sometimes, when he thought nobody was watching. I saw the look in his eyes then. He didn't like it either. It was as though he wore this body, performed these ac-tions, but underneath it. . . .

Do you know what, dearest Kidd? I think, underneath all that bluster, he was *scared*.

1966

I remember that party. 1966, and swinging London had welcomed me with open arms. Dorothea had arranged everything in advance. More and more I was coming to rely on her dedication, her organisational abilities, her total belief. To be so fully believed is a strange and sometimes frightening thing. As a writer I always believed in my creations, for as long as it took to set them down on paper. Once typed and mailed, however, I moved on, to the next story, the next inevitable truth, and the others receded into the past, so that were I challenged, I'd often struggle to remember what it was I had written, or why I had believed in them with such passion— what, indeed, the purpose of writing them at all had been.

I do not know when I became unsatisfied with merely writing. I was always in it for the money, or so I told myself. Heinlein claimed the same. We pictured ourselves as the smart boys, writing because it was easy, and it sure was better than having a working stiff's job. The checks came in the mail. My name was on the cover of the magazines on the racks in the candy stores and the gas stations. People I had never met, nor had any desire to, knew my name, and argued over the most minute details of my stories, in mimeographed "fanzines," which they enthusiastically posted to each other.

At some point it stopped being enough. At some point the whispering shadows came out of the corners and crept against the light, but were they real? Or were they merely an- other story I had told myself? Writers are most easily seduced by their own creations. Were my motivations pure? I had not intended to become an evangelist.

Was I in it, then, simply for the money?

Dorothea had booked me suitable accommodation—a handsome eighteenth-century house in Fitzroy Square—a far cry from the bedsit I stayed in on my first visit to London, after the war, when I had attended a small British convention called a Whitcon, a dour and unglamorous affair upstairs in a pub called the White Hart. There had been around fifty people crammed into the space, then, drinking warm beer and smoking while Arthur C. Clarke droned on about astronautics to anyone who'd listen while eyeing up the boys

Now, London was changed. The grey of the post-war years and the devastation of German bombs were all but gone, and an old-new city emerged, bright, energetic, free. The hippies were drawn to my Lode Stars, seeing in them . . . well, who could say for sure? A metaphor, a promise. We were all on a trip, I told them, a one-way trip to God. And they loved it.

I got laid every night.

I was busy giving lectures. Talking about the future. But I dropped in to that party at Mike Moorcock's flat, I can't say why, exactly. He was a bearded and unkempt young man, full of nervous energy, high on who knew what drugs, full of what he thought were new ideas. I guess I wanted to show off. Perhaps I was just looking for something familiar, but all I could see that night was how far I'd come, how distant I'd become from that comfortable, easy world of the pulps, and the outrageous inventions and petty passions of the world of science fiction.

For a moment I eyed a fellow in a dinner jacket leaning casually against the wall smoking a pipe—Clute, I think his name was, some sort of self-styled critic, an ex-pat Canadian who was with the hippy *New Worlds* crew. I had no time for critics or for hippies, but gave his wife an appreciative up-and-down look-over—she was a cheesecake cutie and no mistake.

The flat was unkempt; there was marijuana smoke everywhere, and everyone who wasn't stoned was drunk; people passed out on the couch or got into fights over Heinlein's

LAVIE TIDHAR

Stranger in a Strange Land; everyone was against pulps, everyone was going to reinvent science fiction, and therefore literature itself, and I was everything they hated—hated and longed to be.

"Gene." I turned at her voice. She was always a striking woman, and now she stood there, regarding me over the rim of her wine glass, and I couldn't read her eyes.

"Judith," I said.

"You remember."

She'd been the wife of my one time agent, Fred Pohl. There had been a bitter divorce and a custody battle—I never cared much for the details. I could think of no earthly reason for her to be in England and I said so. She laughed.

"I am editing an anthology," she said. "*England Rocks SF.*"

"What a terrible title!"

She didn't take offence, to her credit. Her smile turned almost wistful. "You've done well," she said.

"I can't complain."

"Tell me," she said. "Is it everything you wished for?"

"The fame? The money? The women? Is that what you mean?"

"It is."

"It's a good life. But there's more to be done. So much more. I have to tell people. I have to make them see."

"My God," she said. "Don't tell me you're serious."

"You don't believe me?"

"I've known too many writers," she said, "to believe anything they say is true."

"You do not write anymore? Yourself?"

Her smile was guarded. "Sometimes."

"This is my life's work," I told her. She shook her head.

216

"Oh, I don't doubt that," she said.

"Then. . . ."

"You cannot live life as though it were someone else's novel," she said.

People stopped what they were doing, drifted around us. Someone passed me a joint and I took a polite toke and passed it elsewhere. Jim Ballard sat morosely in a corner drinking from a bottle of scotch.

"Life is boring and random and cruel," I said. "Novels are truer."

"True for being a lie?"

"Everything is a lie, Judith. Some lies are just more believable than others."

"I don't know," she said. "Is there anything you believe in? I mean, truly believe, Gene?"

"Do I need to?"

"You and the others. The boys. Robert and Isaac and Fred. All you do is play with toys. You never grew up."

"Listen to the era," I told her. "No one wants to grow up."

"Some of us live in the real world," she said. "There's a war on, or didn't anyone tell you?"

"This is a science fiction world," I told her. "This is the world we made. A world of A-bombs and space rockets, of miracle drugs and scientific marvels. This is our world, Judith!"

I guess I was shouting. The others were all listening, those eager little boys, these pulpsters who wanted to be real writers, who wanted to change the world. As though it were that easy!

"Well, it was good to see you," she said, quietly. There was a buzzing in my head and when I glanced at the sofa it seemed to me that the shadows underneath were growing, that shapeless forms were crawling out of the dark gap, and I could hear, very faintly, the click of hungry mandibles. It was very humid and I was sweating.

I said, "You, too," and meant it. Then I made up some story about a prince or a duke I had to see, and escaped. Outside it was cooler, and a soft rain began to fall. I had gone deeper than I ever intended. The car waited for me outside and the driver opened the door. I got in at the back, with Tiffany or maybe Rachel beside me.

"Where to, sir?" the driver said.

The girl pressed against me. She felt warm and real. I rolled down the window and felt the rain on my face.

"It doesn't matter," I said, tiredly. "Just drive."

"Very good, sir," he said.

32.

1975

"Dad?"

"Yes, Bobbie?"

"Where do people go when they die?"

"You know this, Bobbie. We discussed it in group yesterday."

"We just die? And we break up into atoms and, what did you call them?"

"Quarks, Bobbie."

"And we float around the universe for millions of years as part of other people, or suns, or cosmic dust?"

"All matter came from somewhere. All matter is going somewhere."

"But dad, these black holes—"

"Lode stars, son. Like in my book. Remember?"

"They're like a walnut, right, and the event horizon is the hard shell that protects them, but inside there's something else, hiding, a secret."

"A singularity, Bobbie. It's the place where the laws of physics no longer work. Where the physical universe ends."

"And that's where God is?"

"No. God is outside the universe, watching. You, me, everything is information, everything becomes light that filters into God's scattered eyes. Sooner or later, in millions or billions of years, everything in the universe will compress back into the mass of a bla—of a lode star, son. Sooner or later, you, me, everybody, will be seen by God. God's waiting for us. God's made this universe so it could give life to something like us."

"But Dad?"

"Yes, Bobbie?"

"Is this really real? I mean—"

"Would I lie to you, son?"

"No, of course not—"

"You're my son, and I love you. People need to believe in something, Bobbie. Do you know what religion is, Bobbie? It is the sigh of the oppressed creature, the heart of a heartless world. Do you know who said that?"

"Uncle Bob?"

"No, not fucking Heinlein—look, I didn't mean to swear. It was Karl Marx who said that, Bobbie."

"Who?"

"It doesn't matter. What I'm trying to say to you is that— look. It gives comfort. It's a story, everything is a story. Without stories we can't really be human."

"I don't think I get it, Dad."

"You're making excellent progress, Bobbie. I'm very proud of you. We all are."

"Dad—you know Linda? The girl I liked?"

"I don't recall—"

"Why did you send her off the ship?"

"She just wasn't ready for the truth, Bobbie."

"But I liked her, Dad."

"And one day you'll find the right person, Bobbie. One day, all of this could be yours."

"But Dad—I told you. I want to be a pilot."

"Don't be ridiculous, Bobbie."

"Ok, Dad."

"You're a good boy."

"Ok, Dad."

I remember that evening. We were on board the Prometheus, my flagship, we'd been sailing ever since the IRS began to come after me for unpaid taxes. We were somewhere in the Bahamas, I think, anchored off Nassau, with the sea as calm and flat as glass. It was a moonlit night. I avoided moonless nights, without the sun's light reflected in the moon the nights were too full of stars, too many stars, though Bobbie had been a keen stargazer. More and more, Dorothea ran the organisation from California, though the IRS kept denying our request to be recognised as a bona fide church and thus exempt us from having to pay tax. Sometimes I missed the old days, banging out yarns at a penny a word, telling stories for the story's own sake, for entertainment. But I had a message, I had a thing to tell the world. Not just God but the serpents in his Eyes, who would eat us if they could.

Was my physics rigorous? I was never a scientist and all I know is that the more they claim to know the less they do. If they can't see something they call it Dark, as though that is explanation enough for everything. I wanted to make them *see*.

The church had grown beyond my ability to manage it. The '60s had been a decade of questing for truth in which everything was possible. I devised methods of Occlusion, as I called them, simple mental arithmetic to protect a mind from the parasites of the future, the eaters I could sense all around me. Only the people at the very top knew my real fears—that we were already living within the event horizon, that we were being consumed, reassembled from light only to be devoured like delicacies. People would believe anything.

Not Bobbie, though. Not Robert Charles Hartley, my son, my beautiful baby boy. On board ship he often fell sick. He swam poorly. He picked inappropriate companions, like that girl, Linda, who only befriended him to get close to me. I had her sent back for retraining at the Miami facility, where troublemakers were now usually sent. My poor, brave, beautiful boy. He wasn't cut for the life, he didn't have my gifts but he inherited all my fears. As a young boy he cried in the night, telling me he could see the eaters. I should have known then he was just looking for my affection, my attention, but I was too blinkered and the '70s were a heady era for me, in which I could do anything and everything was possible. I was rich! Richer and more powerful than I'd ever imagined possible. We lived on board the yacht and sailed the ocean, going anywhere we pleased, doing anything we fancied.

Yet Bobbie wanted to leave.

That night, on the deck, with the full moon reflecting in the sea and the lights of the town in the distance, I hugged him close to me.

"You know I love you," I said.

"Yes, Dad. I love you too."

"I want you to try real hard, Bobbie. You are not just anyone. You are Eugene Hartley's son. You must remember that, always."

"I know, Dad. I'll try."

He was a good-looking kid, my boy. A couple of years later he left the yacht to go on holiday back in the States and, in a car park outside a Vegas hotel, he killed himself.

Damn you, Bobbie! Why did you do that to me, you stupid fucking kid?

33.

2001

Once there was a man who fell into the eye of God, and he became a little boy. This is how it starts, or how it ends, I can no longer recall. This is just a story I used to tell myself when I was little.

I forgot the story for a while. But I remembered it on Leserser, on that long, dark year in the South Pacific with only the terrible stars for company. It began to come back to me then. A child's daydream, nothing more. But it didn't give me comfort, during the war: instead, it made me afraid.

If you ask my disciples, they'd tell you that I really did come from the future: from a time and a place so unimaginably far from here that time and space themselves have lost their meaning. They would tell you that I was the messiah, come back from the stars with a message of hope.

My book, the Church believes, is no mere novel. It is the

representation of an interlocking system of ideas, a complex mathematical formula fashioned at the end of time.

Think of it as a sort of benevolent virus. It can copy itself from person to person, providing a sort of protection against the eaters who inhabit God's eyes.

It is what we call an Occlude.

This knowledge is of course only shared at the highest levels of the Church. The mere initiates, the Sacrifice, are given only the bare bones of the story, just enough to draw them in, to offer hope, the promise of salvation.

Isn't that what all religion essentially is?

But ours is couched in the language of science, of study.

Did I ever believe it? Do I believe it now?

I'm not honestly sure that I know.

After my son died, life on board the yacht lost its appeal. It did not happen the next day, or the day after, but gradually, until I woke up one morning, stared out of the porthole of my cabin, and saw nothing beyond: no sea, no sky, no islands, no trees, no life. Nothing but a great barren silence.

The next day I packed my few belongings and flew back to the US mainland. Peggy, my wife, was running most of the Church's mainland operations at that time. She was a hard, ambitious woman. Too ambitious, perhaps. A black flag op she ran against the IRS—the bastards were still after my money—went bad. There is little point going into the finer details of Operation Red Riding Hood; suffice it to say, someone had to go on trial and Peggy was in charge. I had to make an example of her and, thankfully, Dorothea stepped in to manage of everything. In the event, anyway, Peggy only got a year in jail.

By then I could no longer remember if I had ever believed

in the story I so often told. Heinlein died and Asimov followed suit shortly after, and I realised I missed my old friends. The Church kept growing and there was never any shortage of willing recruits. I was richer than anyone had any reason to be. I could go anywhere and do anything.

Instead I left.

The view from my window is beautiful. I spend hours watching the distant mountains, their peaks dusted with snow. The sky never ends here, and at night I can hear the coyotes howl in the desert, under the cold bright stars. This used to be a busy place, but now there's mostly only me. Sometimes I take the beat-up old pickup truck to the nearby town and stock up on groceries, else there's a guy who comes every now and then with the stuff. Most of the time there's just me, a couple of Underwood typewriters, and all the paper I'll ever need. Dorothea knows not to disturb me.

It's peaceful here; and peace, I have learned, is a hard thing to come by: wherever in the universe you may be.

PART SIX

UNLAND

34.

The flight from London to the States was uneventful. I sat pressed against the window, looking out at the clear blue sky that was endless.

I stared at the postcard in my hand.

Dear Daniel,

Time moves differently for me than it did in my old dispensation. The nights stretch to infinity, and beyond the canopy of stars I think in vain that I can see the day break. If Levi was right, if this book which he was so obsessed with really was a sort of alien device, then I or anyone who had come into contact with the thing is now supposedly Occluded—protected from the attention of the naturally evolved parasites who live beyond the event horizon of the black hole.

If he was right, then we are billions of years old, re-created from the last rays of light in the universe, well on our way into the singularity at the black hole's heart, well on our way to being seen by God.

It seems to me a strangely comforting thought, regardless of its validity.

There was a little ink spot under that penultimate line, as though its author had debated for some time how to finish, and the point of the pen had rested on the page until the ink leaked. Then it simply said:

It is beautiful here.

I turned the postcard over, as I had countless times by now.

It was old and worn out, with water damage and a coffee ring left on its front. It showed an amusement park, with the requisite roller coaster ride and a medium-sized Ferris wheel and a bumper car arena. The place was lit up with coloured bulbs and there were mountains in the distance and the beginning of a mesa or desert.

Holding it, I could imagine the smell of candyfloss, the hiss of open gas flames, the taste of popcorn and salt, the shouts and cries of children and the strained smiles of their parents.

The lettering said *Funland Amusement Park and Campground, Montana.*

When I finally landed in Montana it was a couple of layovers and twenty-four hours later.

I was filled with a caffeine-induced, nervous energy. I felt as though I had landed on another alien world. Everyone's voices were strange and the sun was too bright, the very quality of the light had changed.

I approached the car rental service desk. I said, "Excuse me, I have a car booked—"

A woman stood next to me against the counter. I had interrupted. She was arguing with the car rental employee.

"But I am sure it was booked," she said, frowning, "really, you must check again."

I could *see* her frown. I could *see* her face, which was extraordinary, for somehow the different features all came together in a distinct way to form an image my brain could process. I could not *describe* it. Like staring through misted glass that suddenly cleared. Her voice was pure and strong and she had the hint of an accent I couldn't place, as though she came from somewhere that wasn't quite real.

"Sir, if you could wait just a minute," the car rental employee said to me, and tapped keys on his computer. "Where did you say you were going, again?"

"Preston," I said, then realised the question was addressed to the woman beside me, and that she said the same name at exactly the same time as me.

"To Funland, actually," I said, to fill the awkward silence. "The amusement park. Have you heard of it?"

"I can't say that I have, sir."

The woman looked at me as though puzzled.

"Do I know you?" she said.

"I don't. . . ."

I was discomfited by her stare.

"Your name, sir?" the clerk said.

"Chase," I said. "Daniel Chase."

"I have a booking for you, but not," the clerk said, turning to the woman, "for you, miss. You're not on the system. I'm sorry. We're fully booked, as it happens. I can only apologise. . . ."

The woman continued to look at me, searching my face for something. I didn't know what.

"You are going *there?*" she said.

"Yes. It's a . . . I suppose it's a bit of a pilgrimage." I laughed, uncomfortable.

"I am not on the system," she said. "Daniel."

I found her quite disconcerting. There was something in her eyes.

"We could travel together," I said. I didn't know why I said it. I felt compelled to, somehow.

"Daniel," she said. As though my name was a rare and exotic thing.

"Yes."

She stared at me for long moment, thinking.

"I'm Ledia."

She said the name as though reaching some sort of decision.

I extended my hand, automatically, for a shake. She looked at it quizzically until I let my arm drop.

"Well?" she said.

"Well, what?"

"Shall we go?"

I negotiated the keys and the forms in a sort of daydream. We picked the car up on the tarmac outside, a Cadillac convertible, and drove away with the roof down, the sun on our faces and the wind in our hair. "It's like a movie," I told her.

"A what?" she said.

We stopped for lunch at a roadside diner and had milkshakes with our burgers. For me this was a novel experience, and Ledia seemed like she, too, had never been to an American diner before, and chewed her food with a sort of bemused curiosity.

She said little, and when I asked her about her journey she just shrugged. I got the sense she had travelled a long way to get here.

We got back in the car and drove as the landscape changed, became drier and more desolate, until we reached at last the small, sedate town of Preston. We drove down Main Street, past a two-storey hotel and a grocery store and a gun store and two cafés and then, before we quite knew it, we were past the town and on the open road.

"Turn there," Ledia said, pointing, and I saw the crude, painted sign that said FUNLAND, with an arrow pointing down a narrow dirt track. We follow the track, as the shrubbery thinned and then disappeared and the dirt road turned to sand. Then we crested a low hill and the camp was just there, immediately before us.

I idled the car and let it slide slowly forward, down the low hill towards the gate. The ironwork was rusted and the *F* had dropped off entirely at some point in the distant past, and the sign just read UNLAND.

The rollercoaster sat forlorn against the clear blue sky and the Ferris wheel was lying on its side, half-buried in sand. I stopped the car and we climbed out, looking at this scene of desolation: where the caravan park used to be there was now just a lot of empty, sand-blown space but for the end row, where a solitary caravan still stood, overlooking nothing but desert.

Together, not speaking, we made our way across a vast and empty parking lot, on foot, our steps sending little swirls of dust into the air. The hot sun leaned west across the sky. The caravan that was our apparent destination was not new, but seemed well maintained and clean, incongruous in its environment. A pickup truck was parked diagonally outside it.

When we came to the door we both stopped in unison and look at each other. I didn't know why she was there, any more than why I had made the journey.

"Should I knock?" I said.

"Knock?" Ledia said.

"On the door."

"I see," she said, but I wasn't sure she did. I gathered my courage to knock when the door opened.

A small old man stepped outside. His hair was white but still plentiful, and he smoked an unfiltered cigarette. He stopped when he saw us and took a deep drag on his cigarette and coughed before releasing a plume of smoke into the acrid air.

"You're not the usual guy," he said accusingly.

"Sir?" I said, taken aback.

"The delivery guy. What's his name. Miguel, Mamatas, one of those. Who the hell are you?"

"I'm. . . ." I didn't know what to say. "I'm from England," I said.

"England! London? I've been to London."

"From there, yes."

"Dreadful place," the old man said. "Never stopped raining. Who's the doll?"

"Sir?"

"You," the old man said, pointing his cigarette at Ledia. "Who are you?"

She looked at him for a long moment, as though trying to place him. Scanning his face for clues.

"I'm . . . from somewhere else," she said at last. "Somewhere far away."

"I suppose everyone has to come from somewhere," the old man said grudgingly. "Well, what do you two want?"

"Sir, are you. . . . Did you use to be . . . ?" Now that I was there, I didn't know what to say.

The old man cocked his head as though waiting, then seemed to lose interest.

"Well, come in, come in," he said. "Do you want a beer?"

"A beer? No, thank you."

"I'll have one," Ledia said unexpectedly.

We followed the old man inside, into a spacious caravan with the smell of unwashed clothes and stale cigarette smoke. Two typewriters sat on a folding table, an overflowing ashtray between them. Pages of paper were inserted into both, each half-typed already, with reams of typewritten paper sitting neatly in a corner. There were already a couple of discarded cans of beer on the floor, and the old man went to his refrigerator and took out two more, handing one to Ledia.

"You look like I should know you from somewhere," he said, but then, again, he lost interest, and instead pulled the tab on the can. The beer hissed open and the old man licked the foam as it emerged, then drank and sighed in apparent satisfaction. Ledia, more cautiously, followed his lead.

"Do you like science fiction?" the old man said, enthusiastically. "You, young man, you look the type, yes?"

"Yes?" I said.

"Read this," the old man said, thrusting a manuscript into my hands. It was covered in old coffee rings and cigarette ash. "I've been working on this for several years. A new science fiction novel. It will be my legacy. Look!"

I took it from him. The title page said *The Circumference of the World*. I didn't think it was much of a title. I scanned the page.

> *In the wet season the rain falls in drops as fat as butterflies and the islands singaot to each other across the water in the language of the bubu and tamat, ol olfala blong yumi. . . .*

"It's—" I said, and then I didn't know what else to say and handed it back politely. The old man snatched it from me and fitted it back on the manuscript pile.

"I'm sure it will be wonderful," I said, and felt ashamed.

"My legacy," the old man mumbled. He looked suddenly unwell. Ledia went to him. She helped him sit on the fold-down bed, with a tenderness she had not displayed before. She stroked the old man's hair.

"You've done enough," she said.

"Got to . . . hold them . . . off," he said. "And I'm so tired."

His eyes filled with tears.

"I know," Ledia said.

I knew then I was witness to something private; something that was not meant for me.

"My legacy. . . ." the old man said.

"You can rest now," Ledia said. The old man nodded. But he pulled away from her and, rising, shuffled to the kitchenette. He ran water into a cup wearily, and I saw him palming a handful of pills when he thought he wasn't being observed. The old man swallowed the pills and shuddered, and a moment later the bounce returned to his step. When he turned, he looked surprised to see us.

"How did you get in here?" he said. "You're not the delivery guy. What's his name. Miguel. I'm sure it was Miguel. Who are you?"

"We were just leaving," Ledia said. She took my hand and pulled me away to the door. "Thank you for seeing us."

"I did? Yes, I suppose I did. It was lovely to see you too, my dear, but I am tired now. Perhaps the radio. . . ."

A small battery powered radio hung crookedly from a hook and the old man switched it on. The last fading notes of the Everly Brothers' *All I Have to Do Is Dream* emerged in a tinny monophone before being replaced by an excitable newscaster. As we left the caravan, just before the door shut on us, I thought I heard something impossible: an airplane had just hit the World Trade Centre in New York.

But that couldn't be right, I thought: it must be a radio play, like the old Orson Welles broadcast of *The War of the Worlds* back in '38. And so, reassured, I emerged blinking into the outside world, where the sun now sank low against the distant mountains.

I took one step, and then another, and then I stopped and listened to the quiet. It felt so peaceful there. A sudden gust of wind tore a slip of paper from the ground and tossed it in the air, and when I caught it I saw it was a one-dollar bill. I turned the note over but then, instead of finding the portrait of George Washington on the obverse, which I knew from its distinctive hair and the high white collar, the face that stared back at me was that—and I was sure of it—of Eugene Charles Hartley.

I yelped and almost threw it away as though the note was poisoned.

Then I looked closely, and realised my error—below the

portrait, the legend said *One Funland Dollar*, and of course, it must have been just joke money, something they must have once used in the amusement park when it was still operating. I almost laughed, and then I released the note into the air and the wind snatched it away and then it was gone.

I looked for Ledia but she had walked away, towards the desert, and so I followed her at a run.

When they left I watched them out of the window of the trailer. The boy was chasing after the girl and she slowed down for him. They wandered to the edge of the camp, where the desert started. They stood close to each other with their shoulders touching, in a sort of camaraderie I almost envied. The desert spread out before them, red and foreboding and beautiful, and they stood there as the sun set and the world grew dark and the stars came out, one by one, until they filled the sky from horizon to horizon.

I only saw them in silhouette and they were so small against all that sky.

The boy said something to her, I don't know what. She shook her head and pointed at the sky. I didn't need to hear her voice or see her lips move to know what she said.

The boy followed her gaze.

The girl looked up at the stars, and there was wonder in her eyes.

"They're beautiful," she said.

AFTERWORD

Years ago, I watched a performance of Shakespeare's *A Mid-summer's Night's Dream* at a theatre in London. "Your eyes are lode-stars," says Helena in the play, and I was struck dumb with sudden wonder, and the image of black holes arranged in space, the Eyes, haunted me for the rest of the performance. It would be many years and more than a few drafts later before this novel would finally be completed.

My thanks to Carmelo Rafala for publishing, in 2010, a novelette called "Lode Stars," in which the Eyes first make an appearance; and to Gareth Owens, who told me it felt like there was more to be told.

I was first introduced to the concept of face-blindness, or prosopagnosia, in an article in *Best American Science Writing 2007* written by Joshua Davis, and which makes for a fascinating read.

Lode Stars makes no claim to scientific accuracy, though many of the theories it mentions are real, in the sense that they had been put forward by various scientists at various times. I make no case for their validity or otherwise. The anthropic principle and the fine-tuned universe theory are merely ways of asking why the universe seems so uniquely formed to give rise to human life—though equally, we may just be an incidental by-product of Creation. Lee Smolin's fecund universes theory posits black holes are the real *raison d'être* of the universe, an idea that is strangely compelling. Though black holes have been theorised as far back as the eighteenth century, the name itself was only popularised in the 1960s. It is believed that a supermassive black hole is found at the centre of almost all galaxies, including our own.

The best way to see our galaxy is from a place such as the island of Vanua Lava in the South Pacific, where there is virtually no light pollution. I lived on Vanua Lava for a year, and was haunted by the field of stars overhead on moonless nights, when the galaxy spreads from horizon to horizon.

On this island, in 1944, there was a small contingent of American coastwatchers, based on a hill called Leserser. I undertook the climb there, where the remains of their camp can still be found, including the objects—such as the bottle of wine and the corroded bullet—described in Oskar Lens' display cabinet. The story of the war in Vanuatu fascinated me, a tale in which American ships materialised one day off the coast of Espiritu Santo and began to transform the island into an airbase. To this day one can still find the remains of downed planes in the evergreen forests, or be told of the Japanese submarine that had risen from the water and was destroyed, until, for weeks later, its remnants kept washing onto the shore of Sanara.

For a view of the Second World War in Vanuatu, I recommend Lamont Lindstrom and James Gwero's *Big Wok, Storian Blong Wol Wo Tu Long Vanuatu* (1998), while the fascinating story of the coastwatchers can be found in Ritchie Garrison's memoir, *Task Force 9156 and III Island Command: A Story of a South Pacific Advanced Base During World War II, Efate, New Hebrides* (1983). I'm indebted to Dr Lindstrom for providing me a copy of the latter.

I have always maintained an interest in the history of science fiction's Golden Age, a time in which the dreams of the future we would end up living in were beginning to formulate. The authors of these stories were young, awkward, precocious and idealistic. They were badly paid and unappreciated (but for their own small yet devout following of science fiction readers), yet at their best they seemed capable of changing the world. For a sense of that long-vanished world, I'd recommend Isaac Asimov's *In Memory Yet Green* (1979); Frederik Pohl's *The Way the Future Was* (1978); *Better to Have Loved: The Life of Judith Merril* (2004) by Judith Merril and Emily Pohl-Weary; and too many others to count. Anthony Boucher's 1942 murder mystery, *Rocket to the Morgue*, is a *roman à clef* of the early science fiction scene in prewar California, and fascinating mainly for that reason.

A special thanks to John and Judith Clute, who opened their home to me, listened to me complain about this book for far too long, and let me put them briefly in this novel without asking questions.

The year 2001 has long held a special significance: for decades it stood as the epitome of the future, the beginning of a new millennium filled with untold wonders, where everything was possible. When at last it came, it proved indeed to be a pivotal point in history, though perhaps not quite in the way we had envisioned. I was never a dedicated book "runner," yet over the course of 2001 I too supplemented my income, to some extent, buying and selling books. In coming to write of this period I am struck by how much the world had changed. The large bookshops that dominated London at that time, and many of the specialist stores, are all gone—though books continue to be published and sold, and fans and collectors continue to gather in secretive groups, in dimly-lit pubs no longer filled with the smell of cigarette smoke. . . .

Special thanks are due to Maxim Jakubowski, formerly of Murder One, and Erik Arthur, formerly of the Fantasy Centre, for letting me use their characters in this novel. I miss your bookshops every day.

Nick Read's documentary, *Russia's Toughest Prison: The Condemned* (2014) provided some insight into Lens' life in prison; and Horace Silver's *Judas Pig* (2004) was an eye-opening account of gangster life in London.

Lens' "God Helmet" is real, as is the little toy train in Wells-next-the-Sea; the religion described in this book is, however, entirely imaginary.

Internationally renowned author Lavie Tidhar grew up on a kibbutz in Israel and has lived all over the world, including South Africa, Vanuatu, Laos, and the UK. Tidhar works across genres, combining detective and thriller modes with poetry, science fiction, historical, and autobiographical material.

Tidhar's breakout novel *Central Station* received the John W. Campbell Memorial Award and the Neukom Literary Arts Award; it was nominated for the Arthur C. Clarke and Locus Awards. *Central Station* has been translated into more than ten languages and won a Nebula Award in China. His latest novel in the *Central Station*–verse is *Neom*, which is currently a Locus Award Finalist.

Tidhar's novel *Unholy Land* was a Prix Planète SF winner and was on best-of-the-year lists from *NPR Books*, *Library Journal*, and *Publishers Weekly*. His novel *The Escapement* received the Philip K. Dick Award Special Citation and was a *Publishers Weekly* Top-10 Forthcoming Fantasy Title. Tidhar's other awards include the World Fantasy and British Fantasy Awards for his novel *Osama*, a British Science Fiction Award for Best Nonfiction, and the Jerwood Fiction Uncovered Prize for *A Man Lies Dreaming*.

In addition to his fiction and nonfiction, Tidhar is the editor of the acclaimed *Apex Best of World Science Fiction* series and a columnist for the *Washington Post*. His media appearances include Channel 4 News and BBC London Radio. His speaking appearances include Cambridge University, English PEN, and the Singapore Writers Festival. Tidhar has been a Guest of Honour at book conventions in Japan, Poland, Spain, Germany, Sweden, Denmark, China, and elsewhere. He is currently a visiting professor and writer-in-residence at Richmond, the American International University.

Lavie Tidhar currently resides with his family in London.